Scholastic Children's Books
An imprint of Scholastic Ltd
Euston House, 24 Eversholt Street, London, NW1 1DB, UK
Registered office: Westfield Road, Southam, Warwickshire, CV47 0RA
SCHOLASTIC and associated logos are trademarks and/or
registered trademarks of Scholastic Inc.

The Wrath of the Wicked Wedgie Woman
First published in the US by Scholastic Inc, 2001
Copyright © Dav Pilkey, 2001

The Perilous Plot of Professor Poopypants
First published in the US by Scholastic Inc, 2000
Copyright © Dav Pilkey, 2000

*The Big, Bad Battle of the Bionic Booger Boy Part One: The Night of the
Nasty Nostril Nuggets*
First published in the US by Scholastic Inc, 2003
Copyright © Dav Pilkey, 2003

This edition published by Scholastic, 2018

The right of Dav Pilkey to be identified as the author and illustrator of this work
has been asserted by him.

ISBN 978 1407 19254 3

A CIP catalogue record for this book
is available from the British Library.

All rights reserved.
This book is sold subject to the condition that it shall not,
by way of trade or otherwise, be lent, hired out or otherwise circulated in
any form of binding or cover other than that in which it is published. No
part of this publication may be reproduced, stored in a retrieval system,
or transmitted in any form or by any means (electronic, mechanical,
photocopying, recording or otherwise) without prior
written permission of Scholastic Limited.

Printed by CPI Group (UK) Ltd, Croydon, CR0 4YY
Papers used by Scholastic Children's Books are made
from wood grown in sustainable forests.

1 3 5 7 9 10 8 6 4 2

This is a work of fiction. Names, characters, places, incidents
and dialogues are products of the author's imagination or are used
fictitiously. Any resemblance to actual people, living or dead,
events or locales is entirely coincidental.

www.scholastic.co.uk

Special thanks to:
Devin, Tanner and Adam Long

"Imagination is more important
than knowledge."
Albert Einstein

CHAPTERS

The TRUBBLE WiTH CAPTAIN UNderPAnts

NOW it can BE TOLD !!!!!!!

--A informashonal comic By George and Harold.

Onse upon a time There were Two cool Kids named George and Harold.

We Kick Butt.

Me Too.

BuT They had a mean principLe named MR KRupp.

Come over Here, Bubs!

No way

One time George and Harold Hipnotized MR KRuPP with the 3-D HipNO-RiNG™.

You will oBey our comand.

O.K.

ZAP.

George and Harold made him think he was A GReAT super Hero Named CapTain Underpants.

Look--- I'm CApTAIN UNderPANts!

HA HA HA

It was funny at first, But then mr Krupp Jumped out the Window.

Hey where do you Think your going?

To fight crime, ok?

George and Harold Had to chase After Him So he wouldén't get Killed and hurt.

Come over Here, Bub!

No WAY!

They had many advenchures with Lots of inapropreate HUMOR.

DIApers and TOILETS and poop... OH my!

Then one day MR Krupp Askidentelly drank super Juice.

super power Juice

GLUB GLUB

Now He gots super powers. He can FLY Too!

TRA-LA Laaaaa!!!

Two things you half to be careful about is: water _and_ finger snaps.

H2O

SNAP

FOR IF YOU SNAP YOUR FINGERS by MR KRUPP...

SNAP

...He turns into Captain Underpants.

TRA-LA LAAAAA!

And if you pore water on Captain Underpantses head...

...He turns back into MR KRUPP.

BLAH BLAH BLAH

So... If you see MR Krupp, don't snap your fingers or you'll be sorry.

SNAP

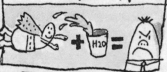

And if you see Captain Underpants, don't pore no water on his head or youll be SORRYER!!!

H2O

Remember- This is **TOP-SECRET** so don't tell anybody!!!

Treehouse Comix

INC.

CHAPTER 1
GEORGE AND HAROLD

This is George Beard and Harold Hutchins.
George is the kid on the left with the tie
and the flat-top. Harold is the one on the
right with the T-shirt and the bad haircut.
Remember that now.

At most schools, the teachers try to emphasize "the three **R**s" (**R**eading, '**R**iting, and '**R**ithmetic). But George and Harold's teacher Ms Ribble was more concerned with enforcing what she called "the three **S**s" (**S**it down, **S**hut your pie holes, and **S**TOP DRIVING ME CRAZY!)

While this was unfortunate for all of her students, it was especially bad for

George and Harold, because they were very imaginative boys.

You see, imagination was not really encouraged at George and Harold's school – in fact, it was discouraged. "Imagination" would only get you a one-way ticket to the principal's office.

This was sad for George and Harold, because they didn't get straight As, they weren't sports stars, and they could barely walk down the hallway without getting into trouble...

PLEASE GO
PEE-PEE
ON YOUR
SOCKS FOR
WARMTH

...See what I mean?!!?

But George and Harold had one thing
that most of the other folks at Jerome
Horwitz Elementary School didn't have:
Imagination. They were *full* of it! And one
day they would use that imagination to save
the entire human race from being
overthrown by a crazed woman with even
crazier super powers.

But before I can tell you that story, I have
to tell you *this* story...

CHAPTER 2
MS RIBBLE'S BIG NEWS

One fine day, George and Harold's class teacher, Ms Ribble, entered the classroom looking a bit meaner than usual.

"All right, settle down!" shouted Ms Ribble. "I have some bad news: I'm retiring."

"Hooray!" cried the children.

"*Not today!*" snapped Ms Ribble. "At the end of the school year!"

"Aww, *maaaan*," moaned the children.

"But the staff are throwing a retirement party for me today…" said Ms Ribble.

"Hooray!" cried the children.

"…during break," said Ms Ribble.

"Aww, *maaaan*," moaned the children.

"There will be lots of free ice cream!"
said Ms Ribble.

"Hooray!" cried the children.

"My favorite flavour: *chunky tofu*!" said
Ms Ribble.

"Aww, *maaaan*," moaned the children.

"But first," said Ms Ribble, "it's time for
something fun!"

"Hooray!" cried the children.

"You all get to make 'Happy Retirement'
cards for me!" said Ms Ribble.

"Aww, *maaaan*," moaned the children.

16

CHAPTER 3

WHEN YOU CARE ENOUGH TO SEND THE VERY BEST

Ms Ribble went around the classroom handing out envelopes, sheets of paper and butterfly stencils to all of the children. Then she wrote a poem on the chalkboard.

"All right, take out your crayons," said Ms Ribble harshly. "I want you to use stencils to make a yellow butterfly on the front of your cards. When you're done, copy this poem on the inside."

"Can we make up our own poems?" asked Melvin Sneedly.

"*No!*" snapped Ms Ribble.

"Do we have to use stencils?" asked Aaron Mancini.

"YES!" yelled Ms Ribble.

"Can we make our butterflies purple?" asked Stephanie Yarkoff.

"*NO!*" screamed Ms Ribble. "Butterflies are yellow! Everyone knows that!"

While the rest of the class worked on their cards, George and Harold had a better idea.

"Let's make Ms Ribble a comic book instead!" said George.

"Yeah!" said Harold. "We can make it all about her. It'll be cool!"

So that's just what they did.

CHAPTER 4

CAPTAIN UNDERPANTS AND THE WRATH OF THE WICKED WEDGIE WOMAN

By George Beard
And Harold Hutchins

CAPTAIN UNDERPANTS
AND THE WRATH OF THE WICKED WEDGIE WOMAN

Story By George Beard · Pictures By Harold Hutchins

Onse upon a time there was A really mean teacher named Ms Ribble who was very mean.

GRRRRR

I'm Am evil!

She gave us lots of homework and yelled at us all the time.

Read 250 Pages for A test!

AW MAN!

One Time at Chrismas Vacashion she gave everybody 41 Book Reports.

Ho Ho Ho!

DEC. 25

Wake up... It's time to open up your presints!

I cant! I half to do my homework!!!

After chrismas everybody turned in A Big Pile of book Reports.

HAW-HAW HAW!

Then something teriBle Happened.

CRASH

Help!

MS RiBBLE WAS BARied in A mounten of Book Reports

Shes REALLY Most SinSERLY Dead.

No Shes Not. We can Re-Build Her...

DocteR

We can mAke Her better than she WAS. ...Faster... Stronger... eviler!!!

Bionic LEG

Bionic LEG

operating table

Surgen

Bionic Hair

Bionic ARM

Bionic ARM

When MS RIBBLE got out of The hospiteL, She had Bionic Powers.

I will take over The World. HAW HAW HAW!!!

So she made a evil costume.

SNIP SNIP

Her Bionic Beehive Hairdoo opened up to ReveaL a evil wedgie ROBO-CLAW.

OUCHIES!

HAW HAW NoBody CAN stop me now!

inosent ByStander

HELP! wedgie Woman is in The teachers Lounge. She just drANk all The coffee and now shes giving The gym teacher A Killer-weDgie!!!

OH, The HORROR!! She better make A fresh pot!!!

Principel

This LooKS LiKE A JOB FOR...

CAPTAIN UnDERP. ANTS!!

CRASH

What'S the Problem, bub? HeLP it's wedgie womAn!

Principel

So CAPtain UnderPants got into A Big Fight with Wedgie womAn. She tRied to give him A wedgie But...

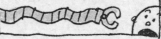

captain UnderPants was Faster than a Speeding waistband...

zip

··· MoRe poweR-FuL Than Boxer Shorts...

OUCH

PoW

And abel to Leap tall bildings without getting A wedgie.

So Wedgie Woman went to the shop to buy some spray starch.

Wedgie Woman sprayed.

OH NO! My underpants is ALL stiff and uncomfortable!

Captain underpants tried to push the buttons on his utility WAistband But they were broke!! He WAS POWERLESS!

SPLASH

Swiming Pool

The KiDS PORED FABRIC SofTener in The PooL.

FABRIC SofTener

Swim

SudenLy The starch got WASHED awAy. HOORAY!!!

my underpants is soft and cottony onse AgAin!!!

HALLy-LooyA!!

Swiming

thanks KidS

No proBLemo.

Soon captain UnderPants Found Wedgie WomAn.

Remember me?

Get Him RoBo-CLAW

NOtise: Any simalarities
to actual persons (living
or dead) is very, very
unforchenate.

CHAPTER 5

THE WRATH OF
MS RIBBLE

When Ms Ribble read the comic book that George and Harold had made, she was furious.

"Boys!" she yelled. "You've just earned yourselves a one-way ticket to the principal's office!"

"But all we did was use our imaginations!" said George.

"You're not allowed to do that in this school!" snapped Ms Ribble. "Didn't you read chapter 1?"

George and Harold gathered their things, and soon they were sitting in the office outside Mr Krupp's door.

"Mr Krupp is on the phone," said the school secretary, Miss Anthrope. "Why don't you boys make yourselves useful and copy the 'Friday Memo' for me! You can pass them out to all the classrooms for me while I go to lunch."

"Aww, *maaaan*!" said George.

"*Quit your whining, buster!*" shouted Miss Anthrope. "I want this done by the time I get back, or you'll *both* be sorry!" Miss Anthrope grabbed her coat and stomped out of the door.

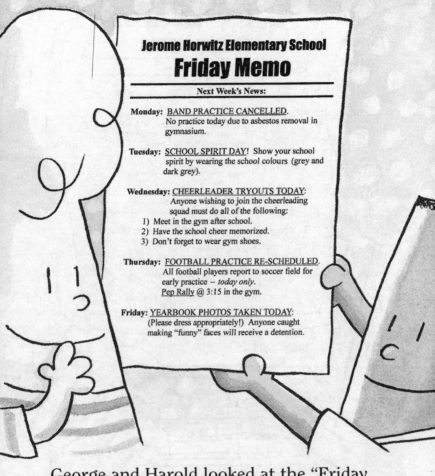

Jerome Horwitz Elementary School
Friday Memo

Next Week's News:

Monday: <u>BAND PRACTICE CANCELLED</u>.
No practice today due to asbestos removal in gymnasium.

Tuesday: <u>SCHOOL SPIRIT DAY</u>! Show your school spirit by wearing the school colours (grey and dark grey).

Wednesday: <u>CHEERLEADER TRYOUTS TODAY</u>:
Anyone wishing to join the cheerleading squad must do all of the following:
1) Meet in the gym after school.
2) Have the school cheer memorized.
3) Don't forget to wear gym shoes.

Thursday: <u>FOOTBALL PRACTICE RE-SCHEDULED</u>.
All football players report to soccer field for early practice – *today only*.
<u>Pep Rally</u> @ 3:15 in the gym.

Friday: <u>YEARBOOK PHOTOS TAKEN TODAY</u>:
(Please dress appropriately!) Anyone caught making "funny" faces will receive a detention.

George and Harold looked at the "Friday Memo". It was a weekly newsletter that told all about the events of the upcoming week.

"Hey," said George. "Miss Anthrope's computer is still on. Y'wanna make a few changes to this newsletter?"

"Why not?" said Harold.

33

Jerome Horwitz Elementary School
Friday Memo

Next Week's News:

Monday: <u>SCHOOL CANCELLED</u>.
No classes today due to lack of interest.

Tuesday: <u>NATIONAL WEAR YOUR PYJAMAS TO SCHOOL AND PICK YOUR NOSE DAY!</u>
Show you care by wearing your pyjamas to school (and picking your nose).

Wednesday: <u>CHEERLEADER TRYOUTS TODAY</u>:
Anyone wishing to join the cheerleading squad must do all of the following:
1) Eat ten whole cloves of raw garlic
2) Draw a moustache on your face with permanent markers.
3) Tape a three-day-old egg-salad sandwich to your head.

Thursday: <u>FOOTBALL PRACTICE RE-SCHEDULED</u>.
All football players report to teachers' lounge for early practice.
<u>Food Fight</u> @ 12:15 in the lunchroom.

Friday: <u>YEARBOOK PHOTOS TAKEN TODAY</u>:
(Please wear Bumblebee costumes.)
Also, whoever makes the funniest face wins a free pizza party for their class.

So George and Harold typed up their own version of the "Jerome Horwitz Elementary School Friday Memo". Then they ran off copies for all the students in the school.

34

CHAPTER 6
THE RETIREMENT CARD

George and Harold were gathering their
new-and-improved "Friday Memo" copies
into small piles when Principal Krupp came
into the office.

"*Hey!*" Mr Krupp shouted. "What are you
two troublemakers doing in here?"

"Miss Anthrope told us to pass the 'Friday
Memo' out to all the classrooms," said
George innocently.

"Well, make it snappy!" yelled Principal
Krupp.

Suddenly, Harold got a sneaky idea. He took out the blank piece of paper that Ms Ribble had given him earlier.

"Hey, Mr Krupp," said Harold, "will you sign this retirement card for our teacher?"

Mr Krupp grabbed the card from Harold and eyed it suspiciously.

"This card is *blank*!" Mr Krupp growled.

"I know," said Harold. "Our class is going to decorate it later. We wanted you to be the first to sign it."

"Well, all right then," said Mr Krupp.
He opened the card and quickly scribbled

Signed, Mr Krupp

on the inside. Then he stormed out of
the office.

"What are you gonna do with that?"
asked George.

"You'll see," said Harold, smiling.

CHAPTER 7
REVERSE PSYCHOLOGY

George and Harold passed out the "Friday Memo" and made it back to their classroom just in time for Ms Ribble's retirement party. George quickly changed the letters around on the sign outside the door, while Harold wrote a special greeting on Mr Krupp's card and stuffed it into the envelope.

"*HEY, BUBS!*" shouted Mr Krupp as he stormed down the hall. "What do you kids think you're doing?"

"We're going to Ms Ribble's retirement party," said George.

"That's what *YOU* think, smart guy!" said Mr Krupp. "Ms Ribble showed me that comic book you boys made about her. And now I catch you changing the letters around on another sign! You boys aren't going to any party ... you're going STRAIGHT to the detention room!"

"Well, *fine*," said Harold. "Then we're not gonna give Ms Ribble the card our class made for her!"

Mr Krupp quickly swiped the card out of Harold's hand.

"A-HA!" he shouted. "I'm going to make SURE she gets this card! I'm going to give it to her *MYSELF*!"

"Aww, *maaaan!*" said Harold.

George and Harold walked down the hallway towards the detention room.

"Wow," said George. "That was pretty cool how you got Mr Krupp to deliver that phony card for you."

"Yep," said Harold. "I used *reverse psychology* on him!"

"I've gotta try that sometime," said George. "By the way, what did you write on that card?"

"You'll see," said Harold, smiling.

CHAPTER 8
THE PARTY

Ms Ribble's retirement party started off bad, and just got worse. First, Ms Ribble forced the class to sing a corny song to her. By the time she was done yelling at the boys for singing off-key, the chunky tofu ice cream was melted.

Everybody had to eat it anyway.

Then the children handed in their "Happy Retirement" cards. Ms Ribble ripped several of the cards up because some of the children had mistakenly drawn polka-dots on their butterflies. One unfortunate boy had also drawn a happy "smiling" sunshine on his card, and he had to stand in the corner.

Finally, Mr Krupp stepped forward and handed Ms Ribble the card he had snatched from Harold's hand.

"I went to a lot of trouble to get this for you," Mr Krupp said gallantly.

Ms Ribble tore the envelope open, and read the card out loud:

"You're One *Hot Mama*!" said Ms Ribble, with a shocked look on her face.

"Eeeeeeeeew!" cried the children.

She opened the card and read the inside.

"Will you marry me? Signed, Mr Krupp."

"Eeeeeeeeeeeeeeeeeeeeeeeeeeeeewww!"
cried the children. The teachers gasped.
Then the room grew silent. Ms Ribble glared
over at Mr Krupp, who had turned bright
red and begun sweating profusely.

He tried to speak. He tried to tell her it
was all a big mistake. He tried to say
SOMETHING... but all that came out was
"B-b-bubba bobba hob-hobba-hobba Wah-
wah."

46

"Er, ummm, *congratulations*," said Mr Meaner, as he patted Mr Krupp's sweaty, shivering shoulder.

"Yes! CONGRATULATIONS!" shouted Miss Anthrope. "This will be the best wedding in the whole world! We can have it here at the school … a week from Saturday! I'll plan everything! You lovebirds don't have to worry about a thing!"

"Er-uh … great … thanks," said Ms
Ribble, still looking quite angry and
confused.

"B-b-bubba bobba hob-hobba-hobba
Wah-wah," said Mr Krupp.

CHAPTER 9
FREAKY WEEKY

The following week at Jerome Horwitz Elementary School was definitely one of the weirdest ones they'd had in a while. For example: none of the kids showed up for school on Monday. But Mr Krupp didn't even seem to notice.

"Hey, where is everybody today?" asked Mr Rected.

"B-b-bubba bobba hob-hobba-hobba Wah-wah," said Mr Krupp.

On Tuesday everybody did show up ... in their pyjamas!

"Why is everybody picking their noses?" asked Miss Fitt.

"B-b-bubba bobba hob-hobba-hobba Wah-wah," said Mr Krupp.

On Wednesday for some strange reason,
the whole school smelled like garlic and
rotten egg-salad sandwiches (especially some
of the girls).

"Boy," said Ms Guided, "the styles today
sure are getting bizarre."

"B-b-bubba bobba hob-hobba-hobba
Wah-wah," said Mr Krupp.

51

Thursday was, without a doubt, a complete and total disaster.

"There's a food fight in the lunchroom!" shouted Mr Rustworthy. "And the football team is destroying the teachers' lounge!"

"B-b-bubba bobba hob-hobba-hobba Wah-wah," said Mr Krupp.

Now, *nobody* was sure what happened on Friday. Apparently there was a mix-up with the dress code and the yearbook photos.

"Our school pictures are ruined!" shouted Ms Dayken.

"B-b-bubba bobba hob-hobba-hobba Wah-wah," said Mr Krupp.

Yes, it was a freaky week, all right. But the big wedding was only a day away … and things were about to get REALLY freaky!

53

CHAPTER 10

THE BIG WEDDING

It was Saturday, the day of the big wedding. Miss Anthrope, true to her word, had taken care of everything. In just one week, she had transformed the gymnasium into a beautiful wedding hall, complete with food, decorations and even a two-metre-tall ice sculpture.

All of the children were dressed in their finest clothes. (Harold even wore a tie!)

"Man," said George, "I can't believe we have to go to school on *SATURDAY*!"

"I know," said Harold. "Why couldn't they have had this wedding during Monday's maths test?"

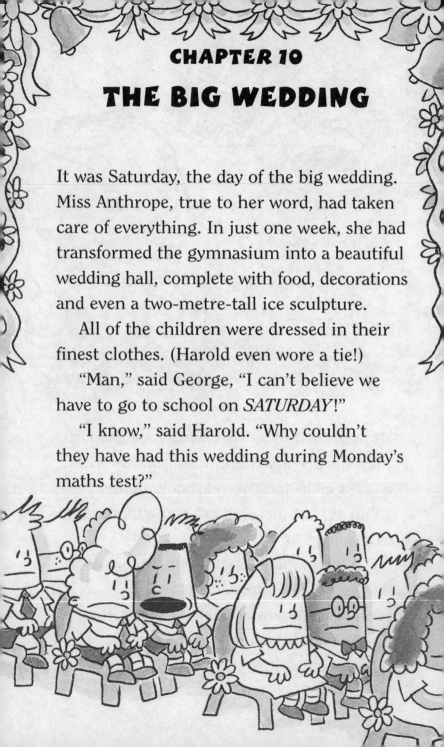

Soon the organist began to play. The rabbi walked down the aisle. He approached George and Harold and stopped to talk to the boys.

"I've heard a lot about you two," said the rabbi, "and I don't want you boys playing any of your tricks today."

"Silly Rabbi," said George, "tricks are for kids!"

Believe it or not, George and Harold had not planned any pranks for the big wedding. They had no "Joy Buzzers" up their sleeves … no squirting flowers in their lapels … and no whoopee cushions on their chairs. They were on their best behaviour. Nothing could go wrong today!

In no time at all, Ms Ribble and Mr Krupp were standing in front of the rabbi, looking quite ill. The rabbi asked Mr Krupp if he would take Ms Ribble to be his lawfully wedded wife.

"B-b-bubba bobba hob-hobba-hobba Wah-wah," said Mr Krupp.

Then the rabbi asked Ms Ribble if she would take Mr Krupp to be her husband.

There was a long silence. Everyone leaned forward. Ms Ribble looked nervously from side to side.

Suddenly, she shouted out at the top of her lungs, "*NOOOOOOOOOOOOOOOO!*"

Ms Ribble turned to Mr Krupp and jabbed her finger into his shoulder. "Listen, Krupp," she said. "I *can't* marry you."

"Hooray! – er, I mean – *aww, that's too bad!*" said Mr Krupp.

"You're a mean, cruel and vicious man," said Ms Ribble, "and I respect that. It's just … it's just…"

"Just what?" asked Mr Krupp.

"It's just your *nose*!" said Ms Ribble. "You've got the most *ridiculous* nose – I've never seen anything quite like it! I just couldn't marry somebody with such a silly nose."

Mr Krupp got angry. "Well, *fine*!" he shouted. "I didn't want to marry you anyway! It was all George and Harold's fault. They *tricked* us!"

Suddenly, everybody in the gymnasium turned and looked at George and Harold.

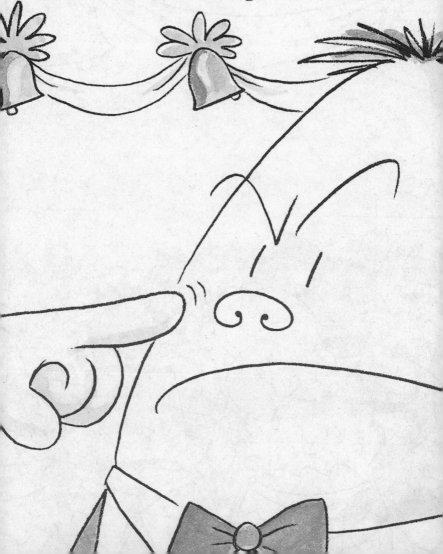

"Time to go," said George.

CHAPTER 11

THE REFRESHMENTS

As George and Harold turned to leave the
gymnasium, they heard the loud thumps of
studded wedding boots clomping down the
aisle towards them.

"I'M GONNA GRIND THOSE KIDS INTO
HEAD CHEESE!" screamed Ms Ribble as
she lunged for the two boys.

George and Harold screamed and ran to the back of the room near the refreshments. There they hid behind two large wooden pillars.

Ms Ribble approached the pillars and grasped them with her mighty hands. With a horrible roar, she pushed the right pillar over. It landed on the back of the luncheon table, causing the front of the table to flip high into the air. Unfortunately, this sent all of the food flying into the crowd.

The creamy candied carrots clobbered
the kindergarteners. The fatty fried fish
fritters flipped on to the first graders. The
sweet-n-sour spaghetti squash splattered the
second graders.

Three thousand thawing thimbleberries thudded the third graders. Five hundred frosted fudgy fruitcakes flogged the fourth graders. And fifty-five fistfuls of fancy French-fried frankfurters flattened the fifth graders.

By now you're probably worried that the wedding guests had nothing to drink with their lovely appetizers. Well, rest assured, the second pillar took care of that. Ms Ribble pushed the left pillar into the fresh fruit display, causing it to topple over, sending

two large watermelons crashing down into
two oversized punch bowls. This created two
enormous splashes of tropical fruit-flavoured
punch, which rained down upon the
wedding guests like a torrential downpour.

Now, no wedding is complete without a
wedding cake. And when Ms Ribble kicked
the ice sculpture over, the resulting crash
sent the beautiful double-deckered cake
flipping high into the air, right over Ms
Ribble's head.

"I'VE GOT YOU NOW!" screamed Ms Ribble, as she grabbed George and Harold by their neckties.

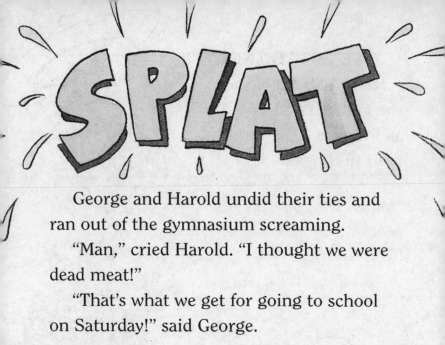

George and Harold undid their ties and ran out of the gymnasium screaming.

"Man," cried Harold. "I thought we were dead meat!"

"That's what we get for going to school on Saturday!" said George.

CHAPTER 12
RIBBLE'S REVENGE

As you might imagine, George and Harold were nervous about going back to class on Monday. But for some strange reason, Ms Ribble seemed happy to see them.

"Good morning, boys," Ms Ribble chirped with a giant, evil, toothy grin. "Come here... I've got something to show you!"

"Uh, oh," said George. "She's smiling – that *can't* be a good sign!"

George and Harold cautiously approached Ms Ribble's desk.

"I took the liberty of adjusting your grades last weekend," said Ms Ribble. "You'll be happy to know that all your grades have just dropped from Bs and Cs to *Fs and Gs*."

"Oh, *NO!*" George gasped. "Not *Fs and Gs!* ... Hey, what's a *G*?"

"It's the only grade *lower* than an *F*!" said Ms Ribble.

"There's no such grade as a *G*," said Harold.

"There is now, bub!" said Ms Ribble. "Looks like you're both going to *FLUNK* the FOURTH GRADE!!! Won't that be fun?"

"No way," said George. "*That's not fair!*"

"Life ain't fair," said Ms Ribble. "Get used to it!"

CHAPTER 13
A BAD IDEA

That afternoon, George and Harold sat in their tree house feeling sorry for themselves.

"She can't get away with that," said George. "We've got to tell somebody about this."

"Nobody's going to believe us," said Harold.

"Well, there is *one* thing we can do," said George. He opened the drawer to their drawing table and searched through the pennies, paper clips, dried spitballs and rubber bands. Then he pulled out a dusty plastic ring with some gum stuck on it. It was the 3-D Hypno-Ring.

"Oh, no!" said Harold. "I thought we threw that thing away!"

"We just threw the instructions away," said George. "But I remember how it works."

"Do you *remember* what happened the LAST TIME WE USED IT?" asked Harold.

"Yeah," said George. "But we were fooling around last time. This time we'll be serious. We won't make any mistakes! All we have to do is hypnotize her into changing our grades back to normal. That's all!"

"I don't know…" said Harold. "It sounds like a bad idea to me!"

"Worse than *FLUNKING* the fourth grade?" asked George.

"Good point," said Harold.

CHAPTER 14

THE RETURN OF THE 3-D HYPNO-RING

The next day at school, George and Harold stayed behind while the rest of the class went outside for break.

"What are you punks still doing here?" asked Ms Ribble.

"Ummmm," said George nervously. "Er, we wanted to show you this really cool ring."

"Yeah," said Harold. "If you look closely at it, you can see a funny picture."

"Well, hold it still," said Ms Ribble, as she stared at the ring intently.

"I have to move it back and forth," said George, "or you won't be able to see the picture."

Ms Ribble's eyes followed the ring back and forth … back and forth … back and forth … back and forth…

"You are getting sleepy," said George.

"Veeery sleepy," said Harold.

Ms Ribble yawned. Her eyes began to droop.

"I'mmssooosleeeeepyyy," she said, as she slowly closed her eyes.

"In a moment," said George, "I will snap my fingers. Then you will be hypnotized."

"Sssssooooosssslllleeeeeeeeepyyyyyyy," mumbled Ms Ribble.

SNAP!

"Now," said Harold, "you must listen very…"

CHAPTER 14½

WE INTERRUPT THIS CHAPTER TO BRING YOU THIS IMPORTANT MESSAGE:

"Hello, This is Chim-Chim Diaperbrains ... er, I mean, this is Ingrid Ashley reporting for Eyewitness News. We have a late-breaking story about a tragic incident that is now occurring in the Pacific Northwest.

"Police have just closed down the Li'l Wiseguy Novelty Company in Walla-Walla, Washington. Apparently, this company has been selling very dangerous 'Hypno-Rings'. We now take you live, via satellite to our reporter, Booger Stinkersquirt, er, I mean, Larry Zarrow, with the latest developments."

"Thanks, Chim-Chim," said Larry. "Reports have poured in from all across the country concerning children who have used the '3-D Hypno-Ring' on their friends and family with disastrous results. But the most shocking revelation is the effect that the rings seem to have on *women*.

"Apparently, whenever the ring is used to hypnotize a woman, a mental blunder occurs, causing the woman to do the OPPOSITE of what she is being hypnotized to do.

"Doctors don't know why the ring causes women to have an OPPOSITE reaction, but they are very concerned. If you or someone you love has purchased a '3-D Hypno-Ring', throw it away at once. And whatever you do, PLEASE DON'T USE IT ON A WOMAN!"

CHAPTER 14³/₄

WE NOW RETURN TO OUR REGULARLY SCHEDULED CHAPTER (ALREADY IN PROGRESS...)

"...and when we snap our fingers," George continued, "you will change our grades back to normal."

"Yeah," said Harold. "And you won't do anything crazy, like turn into *Wedgie Woman*."

"And you won't try to destroy Captain Underpants," said George, "or take over the world, either."

"Right!" said Harold. "You'll just change our grades, and that's it!"

George and Harold looked nervously at each other.

"Well," said George, "I think that covers everything."

"Yep," said Harold. "We shouldn't have any more problems from Ms Ribble."

So the boys snapped their fingers.

SNAP!

CHAPTER 15

BAD HAIR NIGHT

That night, Harold and George camped out in George's tree house.

"I have to drive your mother to work early tomorrow morning," said George's dad. "So you boys are responsible for getting yourselves to school on time."

"OK, Pop," said George.

"We'll be there bright and early, Mr Beard," said Harold.

It had been a tough day for George and Harold, and now it was time to relax. George rolled out the sleeping bags, while Harold unpacked a box of chocolate doughnuts, four cans of orange cream soda, and a big bowl of Bar-B-Q potato crisps. Believe it or not, there was even a cool Japanese monster movie playing on TV.

"You know," said George, "life doesn't get any better than this!"

"Yep," said Harold. "But do you think the Hypno-Ring actually worked on Ms Ribble? She looked a little weird when she came out of her trance."

"Aaah, she was probably just sleepy," said George. "Teachers have very stressful jobs, you know."

"I wonder why?" said Harold.

After the movie, George and Harold
brushed the crumbs out of their sleeping
bags and got ready for bed.

"Let's sleep in our school clothes
tonight," said George. "That way we won't
have to wake up early to get dressed."

"Good idea," said Harold.

So George turned out the light, and soon
the two boys were drifting off to sleep. After
a few minutes, Harold sat up quickly and
looked around.

"Hey!" he whispered. "What's that noise?"

"I didn't hear anything," said George.

They listened closely.

"Shhh!" said Harold. "There it is again!"

George heard it this time. He reached
over and opened the tree house door a crack.
All they could hear was the sound of crickets
chirping in the night. George opened the
door wider, and the boys peeked down.

85

"AAAUUGH!" roared an evil-looking
woman dressed in tight purple vinyl and a
mangy-looking fake-fur boa.

George and Harold screamed in horror!
The snarling woman climbed from the
ladder into the tree house. George and
Harold recognized her immediately in the
moonlight.

"*Ms Ribble,*" George gasped. "What a lovely, uh, *outfit* you have on."

"Who's Ms Ribble?" the angry lady growled. "My name is *Wedgie Woman*!!!"

George and Harold looked at each other and swallowed hard.

"I understand that you boys have information about Captain Underpants," said Wedgie Woman.

"What makes you say that?" asked Harold.

"I've read your comic books," said the evil villain. "You boys know his strengths, his weaknesses, and I'll bet you even know his SECRET IDENTITY!"

"No way!" said George. "Captain Underpants isn't real... He-he's just a cartoon!"

"We'll see about that," Wedgie Woman scoffed.

Wedgie Woman reached out and grasped
George and Harold's arms.

"What do we do now?" cried Harold.

"We can take 'er," said George. "It's not
like she has super powers or anything!"

CHAPTER 16

WHO'S AFRAID OF THE BIG BAD BEEHIVE?

The struggle that followed may someday be remembered as the single most unlucky thing that ever happened in the history of the world.

First, George pulled his arm out of Wedgie Woman's grasp. Then Harold squirmed away, too. When Wedgie Woman lunged after them, George crouched down into a ball behind Wedgie Woman's feet. All it took was a simple nudge from Harold to send the ferocious female toppling over backwards...

...right into the wall. KLUNK! The bookshelf above Wedgie Woman's head shook violently, causing a strange-looking juice carton to topple over. Suddenly, a stream of glowing green juice poured out of the carton, directly into the tightly woven beehive of hair atop Wedgie Woman's head.

"NOOO!" yelled Harold as he grabbed the juice carton. "This is the juice we got from that spaceship back in our third book!"

"You mean the one with the annoyingly long title?" asked George.

"Yeah!" said Harold. "This is EXTRA-STRENGTH SUPER POWER JUICE! And a whole bunch of it got in her hair!"

"Don't worry," said George. "None of it got in her mouth. What's the worst thing that could happen? Her *hairstyle* would have super powers?"

"Well," said Harold, "I guess you're right. That *is* pretty stupid ... even for one of *our* stories!"

"It's pretty funny, though," said George.

Suddenly, two coiled arms of twisting hair shot out of Wedgie Woman's head and grabbed George and Harold by the back of their underwear, yanking them high into the air.

"You know," said George, "this isn't as funny as I thought it would be."

CHAPTER 17
ALL TIED UP

Wedgie Woman brought George and Harold
back to her house and tied the boys tightly
to two chairs.

"Tell me the secret identity of Captain
Underpants!" screamed Wedgie Woman.

"No way!" said George.

"Hmmmm," said Wedgie Woman. "You
want to do this the hard way? *No problem!*"

Wedgie Woman's hair began uncoiling itself. Several twisted locks of hair stretched out into the living room and started taking apart the television, the computer and a Thighmaster®.

Other tangled coils reached into the kitchen and began dismantling the dishwasher, the toaster and a food processor.

"What are you doing?" asked Harold.

"If you want to make robots," said Wedgie Woman, "you gotta break a few small appliances!"

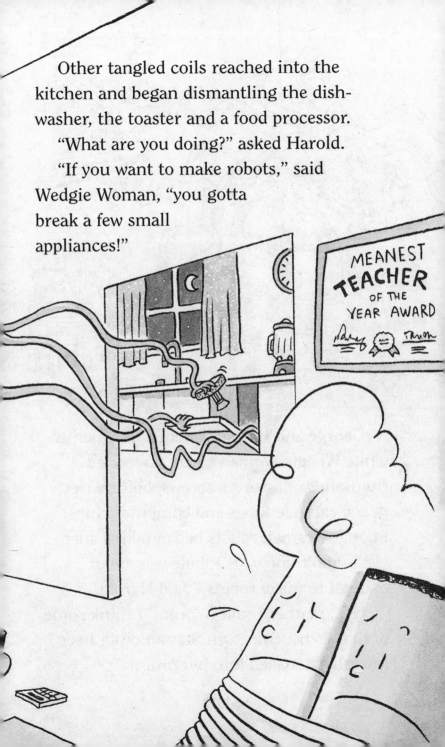

MEANEST
TEACHER
OF THE
YEAR AWARD

George and Harold watched impatiently
while Wedgie Woman's hair assembled
thousands of assorted screws, bolts, wires,
gears, cathode tubes and computer chips.
Soon, two small robots began taking shape.

"I didn't know Ms Ribble was smart
enough to make robots," said Harold.

"Me, neither," said George. "I think some
of that EXTRA-STRENGTH SUPER POWER JUICE
must have soaked into her *brain*!"

The next morning, Wedgie Woman completed her robots, which she named "Robo-George" and "The Harold 2000".

"You know," said Harold, "something about those robots seems a little *familiar*!"

"Yeah," said George. "They kinda look like us ... only not as dashingly handsome."

Wedgie Woman opened the robots' chest plates and inserted a can of spray starch into each one. Then she sealed the chest plates, patted each robot on the head, and sent them both off to school. "Captain Underpants doesn't stand a chance now!" Wedgie Woman laughed.

"Wait a minute," said Harold. "How are those two robots going to stop Captain Underpants?"

"All they have to do is wait and listen," said Wedgie Woman. "And as soon as they hear the words 'Tra-La-Laaaaa!', *it'll all be over*!"

CHAPTER 18

ROBO-GEORGE
AND THE HAROLD 2000

"Uh, attention boys and girls," said Mr
Krupp to the fourth graders. "Your teacher,
Ms Ribble, didn't come to school today."

"Hooray!" shouted the children.

"*Settle down!*" Mr Krupp shouted. "You're
still going to have all your classes!"

"Aww, *maaaan!*" moaned the children.

"But you're going to have a substitute
teacher," said Mr Krupp.

"Hooray!" shouted the children.

"And it's going to be *me*!" said Mr Krupp.

"Aww, *maaaan!*" moaned the children.

The whole day was pretty much like a normal day, except for one thing: Mr Krupp couldn't understand why George and Harold were so well behaved.

They didn't make funny noises during science class, they didn't stick crayons up their noses during art class, and they didn't draw comic books during maths class. In fact, they even walked past a sign without changing the letters around. Mr Krupp was stunned.

"All right, you two!" Mr Krupp shouted. "I know you're up to something... You better stop being so good, or you're gonna be in *BIG TROUBLE*!"

TODAY'S LUNCH

GENETICALLY MODIFIED MEAT FLAVOURED BEEF

WITH EXTRA BOVINE GROWTH HORMONES

But Robo-George and the Harold 2000
kept right on behaving. The only time they
did something even remotely wrong was
during break. Everybody was playing
kickball, and when it was the Harold 2000's
turn to kick the ball, he kicked it pretty darn
hard.

KA-BOINGGG!

101

The kickball tore right through the top of page 101 and out the other side as it sailed towards the outer regions of Earth's atmosphere. Soon it broke free of our planet's gravitational pull and began heading straight towards the planet Uranus.

"A-HA!" shouted Mr Krupp, as he pulled out the official school rulebook and read Rule no. 411 out loud: *It is against the rules to kick school property into outer space! You're in trouble now, bub!*

But the Harold 2000 ignored Mr Krupp
and began running around the bases.

"Hey! I'm talking to you, Hutchins!" Mr
Krupp shouted. He pointed at the Harold
2000 and snapped his fingers.

SNAP!

Suddenly, Mr Krupp began to change.
A silly-looking smile stretched across his
face, and he stood before the fourth graders
looking quite heroic. Quickly, he turned
and ran back into the school.

CHAPTER 19
TRA-LA-LUUUNATICS

Several minutes later, Captain Underpants flew out of Mr Krupp's office window. As the hero zipped across the sky, he let out a triumphant "Tra-La-Laaaaa!"

When Robo-George and the Harold 2000 heard the words "Tra-La-Laaaaa!", they immediately stopped playing kickball. Suddenly, their arms began to extend and their legs stretched towards the sky.

Strange secret compartments in their ever-growing torsos opened up, revealing giant rocket boosters and the latest in advanced aviation technology. Steel panels on their faces and bodies expanded wildly as their complex structures swelled to highly improbable proportions.

Suddenly, flames shot out of their retro-thrusters as their bodies rose into the air. In no time at all, two gigantic robots were flying in hot pursuit of the Amazing Captain Underpants.

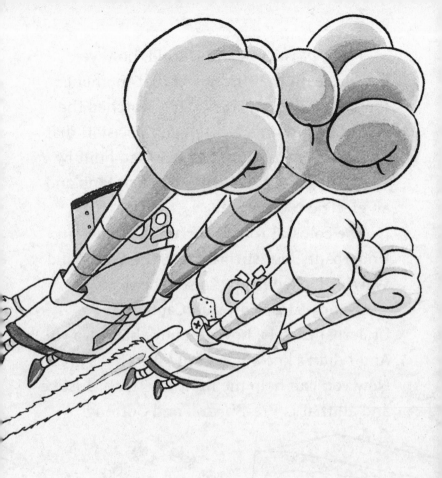

"George and Harold are in BIG trouble now," said Melvin Sneedly, as he read Rule no. 7,734 of Mr Krupp's official school rulebook out loud: *"It is against the rules for students to transform into giant flying robots during afternoon break!"*

The *real* George and Harold, however, had more on their minds at that moment than a few broken rules. They watched the action unfold on a big-screen television that Wedgie Woman's horrible hair had built by combining the spare parts of a fish tank and an electric toothbrush.

The colossal robots surrounded Captain Underpants, but surprisingly, the Waistband Warrior looked happy to see them.

"George! Harold!" said Captain Underpants. "My, how you boys have grown! And I didn't know you could fly. That's great! Now you can help me fight for Truth, Justice and all that is Pre-Shrunk and Cottony!"

LIVE ④

But the gigantic robots didn't respond. Instead, they hovered close to Captain Underpants as their steel chest plates opened up. Suddenly, two extendable robotic arms reached out and began showering Captain Underpants with liquid spray starch.

"What-what are you doing?" cried Captain Underpants. "That's *SPRAY STARCH*! It's the only thing in the world that can take away my super powers!!!"

The Waistband Warrior screamed in horror as he began falling through the sky. Robo-George quickly swooped down, grabbed the helpless hero, and hung him by his waistband on a tall pole high above the city streets.

CHAPTER 20
YOU AXED FOR IT

"Hooray!" cried Wedgie Woman as she turned off her new TV. "My plan worked. Now it's time to take over the world!"

"But what about us?" asked Harold.

"Don't worry," said Wedgie Woman. "I've got a big surprise for you two." She took a heavy battle-axe and tied it up with a rope. Then she leaned the axe towards George and Harold, and lit a candle under the rope.

"When the flame burns through the rope," said Wedgie Woman, "all your problems will be over. Get the point?"

"Not really," said George.

"Don't worry," laughed Wedgie Woman. "You will soon enough."

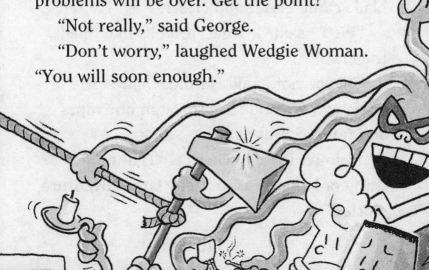

Wedgie Woman laughed a horrible laugh. Then she dashed out of the door to take on the world!

George and Harold watched as the flame began burning through the rope. They cringed as the impending doom of the axe blade came closer and closer.

"Well," said George, "it looks like this is the end."

"Maybe not," said Harold. "Maybe the blade will fall and slice through our ropes and not harm us at all."

"I doubt it," said George. "That kind of thing only happens in really lame adventure stories."

Suddenly, the blade fell and sliced through the ropes, not harming George or Harold at all. The two boys looked at each other and decided it was best not to comment on the situation.

CHAPTER 21

THE WOOTHLESS WEVENGE OF THE WICKED WEDGIE WOMAN

Wedgie Woman headed to the centre of town to meet up with Robo-George and the Harold 2000. "Well done, my precious robots," said Wedgie Woman affectionately.

"What's all this then?" said a policeman who had just arrived on the scene.

"Er – nothing, officer," said Wedgie Woman. "Just the beginning of my TOTAL WORLD DOMINATION!"

"Oh, OK," said the cop. "Hey, *wait a minute*!" But before the police officer could voice his objections, a twisted dreadlock from Wedgie Woman's head shot out and grabbed the cop by the back of his underwear.

The colossal Harold 2000 lifted the officer
and hung him from a stop sign.

"Owie, *WOWIE*!" cried the cop.

Soon more police officers headed to the
scene, but they all met with the same
terrible fate as the first policeman.

116

Before long, every cop in the city was hanging from a street sign.

"Call the National Guard!" screamed the Chief of Police. "Call the Army – call the Marines – call a *HAIRSTYLIST*!"

Soon, the armed forces arrived with a whole fleet of tanks and helicopters. But everybody was afraid to shoot. Wedgie Woman was just too quick.

The giant robots stomped around the city as Wedgie Woman barked out her commands. "Everybody on Earth must obey ME!" cried the Wicked Wedgie Woman. "If anybody refuses, they'll get the WEDGE! If anybody tries to stop me, it's WEDGIE TIME! Bow down to me ... or *WELCOME TO WEDGIEVILLE*!"

Soon George and Harold arrived at the scene. They hid in some bushes and watched the terror unfold.

"We've got to rescue Captain Underpants," whispered George. "He's the only one who can save the world!"

"But how?" whispered Harold. "He's got no super powers left!"

"Sure he does!" said George. "Starch doesn't really take away super powers ... he just *THINKS* it does. We've got to change his mind!"

"I sure hope we can!" said Harold.

CHAPTER 22
THEY CAN'T

George and Harold ran to the pole where the heartbroken hero was hanging.

"Hey, Captain Underpants," cried Harold. "You've got to come down from there and save the city!"

"C-can't," whined the Waistband Warrior. "N-need fabric softener!"

"No you *don't* need fabric softener!" said George sternly. "That was just a dumb joke in one of our comics!"

"But you don't understand," said Captain Underpants. "Starch is the enemy of underwear. Only fabric softener can save me!"

"*RATS!*" said Harold in frustration. "Hey, George, are there any shops around here?"

"Yeah," said George. "A new one just opened down on Oak Street."

"Then let's go buy some fabric softener," said Harold. "It'll be easier than trying to reason with the guy."

"How's that going to help?" asked George.

"It's all in his mind," Harold explained. "If he *believes* that fabric softener will save him, then it probably will. I think it's called 'the Placenta Effect'."

So George and Harold ran to Oak Street. "What's the name of that shop?" asked Harold.

"I can't remember," said George. "I think it's called 'Everything Except ... umm —'"

"Aww, *maaaan*!" said George.

"*We're doomed!*" cried Harold.

"Listen," said George. "We've got to make another comic book!"

"Now?!!?" asked Harold.

"It's our only hope," said George. "The fate of the entire planet is in our hands!"

So the two boys bought some paper and a few pencils, and got down to work.

Twenty-two minutes later, George and
Harold had created an all-new Captain
Underpants adventure. They ran back to the
pole where Captain Underpants was hanging
and tossed their new comic up to him.

"This is no time to be reading comics,"
said Captain Underpants.

"Just read it, bub!" said Harold.

"Yeah," said George. "You might learn
something!"

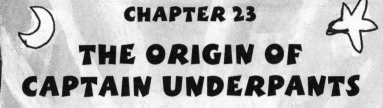

CHAPTER 23
THE ORIGIN OF CAPTAIN UNDERPANTS

THE True **UNTOLD** Story!

By George Beard
and
Harold Hutchins

THE ORIJIN OF CAPTAIN UNDERPANTS

the TRUE UNTOLD STORY BY G. BEard and H. Hutchi...

A far time Ago in a Galaxy Long, Long Away...

...there WAS A Planet Called Underpantyworld.

Underpantyworld WAS A peaseful planet where everybody wore only Underwear.

HA Ha I can see your Underwear.

Hey What are you doing under there?

Under where?

I can see yours to. Ha Ha Ha

Ha Ha You SAid "Underwear"

Ha Ha

EveryBody Liked Wearing Underwear so much that they never got into Fights and they dident have no wars either. It WAS Cool.

Don't worry. I have a maJic Amyoulet that will protect us from starcH!

Yipee!

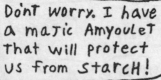

But he Acksidentelly dropped The maJic Amyoulet.

oopsies.

It fell into the mouth of his newborn son, "Little Baby Underpants."

GULP.

OH NO--- He swallowed it! We're Are Doomed

Just then the Wedgie WARLoRds sprayed starch on Underpantyworld.

WW

STARCH SHIP Enterprize

Sssssssss

BiG Daddy Long Johns and his lovely wife "Princess Pantyhose" knew that there planet was a goner. So they desided to save there baby.

So they stretched his underwear real far.

STRECH

Then they let go and shot him into space.

ZING

weeeee

Be Good!

Don't pick Your nose!

Little Baby Underpants SAiled Threw Space as his home planet Crumbled behind him.

AW, MAN

BOOM

Soon Little BABy Underpants FELL To Earth.

BONK

WELCOME TO EARTH

Little Baby got Adopted by some old guys.

my he's So CUTE

LETS Adop him

O.K.

They named him "Captain" After there Faverite Cereal.

Hi "Captain"

Hi

CAPT CRUN

BUT as the years went by, Captain Became very Sad. For some STRANGE reason, he never ever seemed to Fit in.

Why do I feel So diferent?

CHAPTER 24
THE PLACENTA EFFECT

"Wow," said Captain Underpants. "I didn't realize that I had the power within me all along to overcome the evils of starch."

"JUST SAY THE WORDS!" shouted George and Harold.

"OK," said Captain Underpants. "But I think it's a great metaphor for—"

"JUST SAY THE WORDS!" yelled George and Harold.

"*All right!*" said Captain Underpants. "But all I'm saying is that—"

"*JUST SAY THE WORDS!*" screamed George and Harold.

"You know," said Captain Underpants, "you kids have *NO* feel for dramatic tension!" Then he cleared his throat and spoke in a powerful voice. "I SUMMON THE POWER OF UNDERPANTYWORLD!"

Suddenly, Captain Underpants rose triumphantly into the air. He was free at last!

When the gigantic robots saw that
Captain Underpants had escaped, the Harold
2000 launched its rocket arms at our hero.

Captain Underpants grabbed the giant robo-arms and swung them around towards his foes.

"These might come in handy," said the Waistband Warrior.

CHAPTER 25

THE INCREDIBLY GRAPHIC VIOLENCE CHAPTER (IN FLIP-O-RAMA™)

WARNING:

The following chapter contains
scenes that are so violent
and naughty, you aren't
allowed to view them.

We're not kidding.

DO NOT READ
THE FOLLOWING CHAPTER!
Don't even look at it.
Just skip ahead to page 156,
and don't ask any questions.

P.S. Don't breathe on it, either.

PILKEY® BRAND

D·RAMA

HERE'S HOW IT WORKS!

STEP 1

First, give yourself eleven spankings. Then, place your *left* hand inside the dotted lines marked "LEFT HAND HERE" Hold the book open *flat*.

STEP 2

Grasp the *right-hand* page with your right thumb and index finger (inside the dotted lines marked "RIGHT THUMB HERE").

STEP 3

Now *quickly* flip the right-hand page back and forth until the picture appears to be *animated*.

(For extra fun, try adding your own sound-effects!)

FLIP-O-RAMA 1

(pages 141 and 143)

Remember, flip *only* page 141.
While you are flipping, be sure you
can see the picture on page 141
and the one on page 143.
If you flip quickly, the two
pictures will start to look like
<u>one</u> *animated* picture.

Don't forget to
add your own sound-effects!

LEFT HAND HERE

ROUGHIN' UP
THE ROBO-GEORGE

RIGHT
THUMB
HERE

RIGHT
INDEX
FINGER
HERE

ROUGHIN' UP
THE ROBO-GEORGE

FLIP-O-RAMA 2

(pages 145 and 147)

Remember, flip *only* page 145.
While you are flipping, be sure you
can see the picture on page 145
and the one on page 147.
If you flip quickly, the two
pictures will start to look like
<u>one</u> *animated* picture.

Don't forget to
add your own sound-effects!

LEFT HAND HERE

HORRIBLY HURTIN'
THE HAROLD 2000

RIGHT
THUMB
HERE

RIGHT
INDEX
FINGER
HERE

HORRIBLY HURTIN'
THE HAROLD 2000

FLIP-O-RAMA 3

(pages 149 and 151)

Remember, flip *only* page 149.
While you are flipping, be sure you
can see the picture on page 149
and the one on page 151.
If you flip quickly, the two
pictures will start to look like
<u>one</u> *animated* picture.

Don't forget to
add your own sound-effects!

LEFT HAND HERE

LET'S PUT
OUR HEADS
TOGETHER

149

RIGHT THUMB HERE

RIGHT
INDEX
FINGER
HERE

150

LET'S PUT
OUR HEADS
TOGETHER

FLIP-O-RAMA 4

(pages 153 and 155)

Remember, flip *only* page 153.
While you are flipping, be sure you
can see the picture on page 153
and the one on page 155.
If you flip quickly, the two
pictures will start to look like
<u>one</u> *animated* picture.

Don't forget to
add your own sound-effects!

LEFT HAND HERE

THE SUPER-SMASHY
CYBER SLAM

153

RIGHT
THUMB
HERE

RIGHT
INDEX
FINGER
HERE

154

THE SUPER-SMASHY
CYBER SLAM

156

CHAPTER 26

REVERSE PSYCHOLOGY 2

The giant robots were defeated, but the battle was not over yet. Harold ran back to their tree house to grab the 3-D Hypno-Ring, while George ran back to Everything Except Fabric Softener for some more supplies.

Soon George returned to the centre of town carrying a big cardboard box filled with spray cans.

"What are you doing with that?" asked Harold, who had just arrived with the 3-D Hypno-Ring.

"I'm taking this *Extra-Strength Spray Starch* someplace where Wedgie Woman won't be able to find it!" George shouted rather loudly.

"Extra-Strength Spray Starch?" cried the
Wicked Wedgie Woman. "That's just what I
need!" Her winding hair lashed out at
George, stopping him dead in his tracks.
Then nine twisting braids each grabbed a
can from the box and began spraying them
at Captain Underpants.

159

A huge cloud of mist filled the air, covering everything in sight, and making these two pages incredibly easy to draw.

When the cloud finally lifted, all of Wedgie Woman's hair was gone. In fact, all of EVERYBODY'S hair was gone.

"See?" George explained. "There was no spray starch in this box. This box was just a cleverly disguised carton of hair remover. I used *reverse psychology* on her."

"Aaugh!" screamed Harold, as he clutched his bald head. "My mum's gonna lay hard-boiled eggs when she sees me!"

"Relax," said George. "Our hair will grow back!"

"That's easy for you to say," said Harold. "Your hair was only a centimetre long!"

CHAPTER 27

REVERSE REVERSE PSYCHOLOGY

"Well, Wedgie Woman," said Captain Underpants. "It's off to jail with you!"

"Wait a second," said Harold. "We'll take care of Wedgie Woman. You go back to the school, put some clothes on, then wash your face."

"Yeah, bub," said George. "Use plenty of water! We've got work to do."

"OK," said Captain Underpants.

So Captain Underpants did as he was
told, and in no time at all he was back to
his Kruppy old self. It was now time to
transform Wedgie Woman back to her old
self, too ... *with some slight modifications*.

"OK," said Harold, "remember when we
hypnotized Ms Ribble, and she did the
opposite of everything we wanted her to do?"

"Yeah," said George.

"Well, if we want to set things right,"
Harold continued, "we've got to hypnotize
her into doing the *opposite* of the opposite
of what we want."

"I'm way ahead of you," said George.

So the two boys once again hypnotized their teacher. Only this time, they used reverse *reverse* psychology on her.

"From now on," said George, "you will ALWAYS be known as Wedgie Woman."

"You WILL keep all your super powers, too," said Harold.

"You WILL NOT go back to teaching fourth grade," said George.

"You WILL remember everything that happened in the last two weeks," said Harold.

"You WILL NOT change our grades back to normal," said George.

"You WILL NOT become the nicest teacher in the history of Jerome Horwitz Elementary School," said Harold.

"And you WILL NOT bake fresh chocolate chip cookies for our class every day," said George.

"*George!*" said Harold sternly. "Stop goofing around!"

"I can't help it," said George. "You should never hypnotize anybody when you're hungry!"

"OK, OK," said Harold. "Let's just snap our fingers and PRAY that this works."

SNAP!

CHAPTER 28

TO MAKE A LONG STORY SHORT

It did.

CHAPTER 29
BETTER LIVING THROUGH HYPNOSIS

The next day, Ms Ribble entered the classroom looking a whole lot friendlier than usual.

"Boys and girls," said Ms Ribble, "I have some good news for you."

"Hooray!" cried the children.

"It's time for English class," said Ms Ribble.

"Aww, *maaaan*," moaned the children.

"Today," said Ms Ribble, "I've asked George and Harold to lead the class."

"Hooray!" cried the children.

"They're going to teach us about creative writing…" said Ms Ribble.

"Aww, *maaaan*," moaned the children.

"…by showing us how to make our own comic books!" said Ms Ribble.

"Hooray!" cried the children.

"While they're doing that," said Ms Ribble, "I'm going to pass out something for you all to work on…"

"Aww, *maaaan*," moaned the children.

"...homemade chocolate chip cookies!" said Ms Ribble.

"Hooray!" cried the children.

"This is awesome," said Harold, "but do you think it was right for us to change her personality like we did?"

"Sure, why not?" said George. "She's happier. She'll probably live longer!"

"You're right," said Harold. "I guess hypnosis is a pretty cool thing sometimes."

Then again (as we all know) sometimes it isn't.

"OH, NO!" screamed Harold.

"Here we go again!" screamed George.

FOR BUTTERCUP GIZZARDSNIFFER WITH LOVE

CHAPTERS

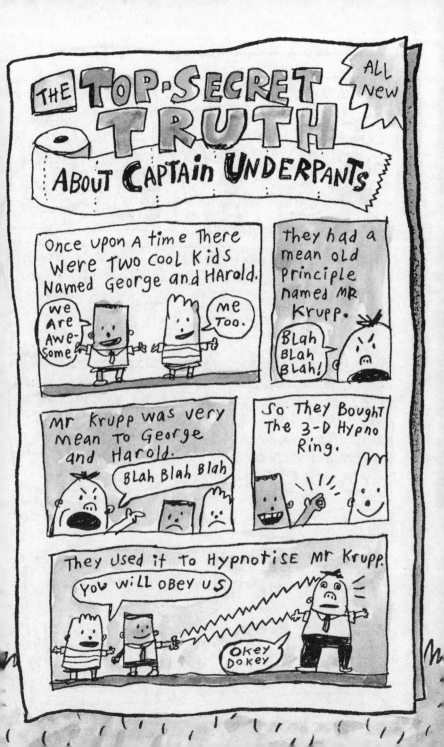

But They Made A Terible MisTeak.

You Are now CAPTAIN Underpants

HA HA

O.K.

Hey! come bACK MR. KRUPP!

TRA-LA LAAAA

MR KRUPP Thought he realy WAS CAPTain Underpants... But he dident have Any Super powers.

STOP

You big dummy

They hAd a Lot oF advenchers. One time they even got ATTACKED By A U.F.O.!!!

UH, OH!

They ALL got Took into The SPACE ShiP... And George stole Some ALien "Super power Juice."

Then Mr. KrUPP got EaTen by A big evil DandyLion.

...you HAd to be there.

So George gave him Some "Super Power Juice"

Then he got super powers!

Now Captain Underpants Has Amazing strength He can even **FLY** too.

HOLY COW

The only way George And Harold can Stop Captain Underpants From Causing troubel is by Poring water on His head...

... This makes him Turn Back into mr. Krupp.

Hey, BUB

But Beware: Because whenever Mr. Krupp Hears somebody snap there fingers...

SNAP **SNAP**

... He turns back into "You-Know-Who."

TRA-LA-LAAAAA!!!

OH, NO!

Here we Go Again

THE END?

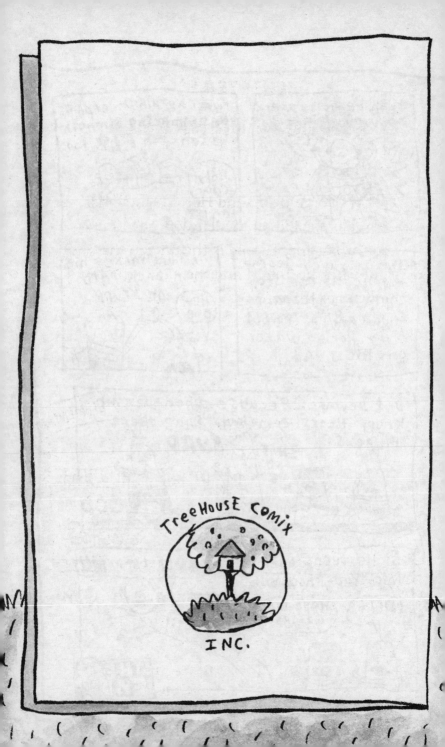

TreeHousE comix

INC.

CHAPTER 1

GEORGE AND HAROLD

This is George Beard and Harold Hutchins.
George is the kid on the left with the tie
and the flat-top. Harold is the one on the
right with the T-shirt and the bad haircut.
Remember that now.

All of the "experts" at Jerome Horwitz Elementary School had their opinions about George and Harold. Their guidance counsellor, Mr Rected, thought the boys suffered from A.D.D. The school psychologist, Miss Labler, diagnosed them with A.D.H.D. And their mean old principal, Mr Krupp, thought they were just plain old *B.A.D.*!

But if you ask me, George and Harold simply suffered from I.B.S.S. (Incredibly Boring School Syndrome).

You see, George and Harold weren't really bad kids. They were actually very bright, good-natured boys. Their only problem was that they were bored in school. So they took it upon themselves to "liven things up" for everybody. Wasn't that thoughtful of them?

Unfortunately, George and Harold's *thoughtfulness* got them into trouble every now and then. Sometimes it got them into a *LOT* of trouble. And one time it got them into *so much* trouble, it almost caused the entire planet to be taken over by a ruthless, maniacal, mad-scientist guy in a giant robot suit!

But before I can tell you that story, I have to tell you *this* story...

CHAPTER 2
ALL HAIL NEW SWISSLAND

As everybody knows, New Swissland
is a small country just south-east of
Greenland. You probably know all about
New Swissland's natural resources and
systems of government. But here's
something about New Swissland that I'll
bet you didn't know: everybody in New
Swissland has a silly name.

Just ask their president, the Honourable
Chuckles Jingleberry McMonkeyburger Jr.
or his lovely wife, Stinky.

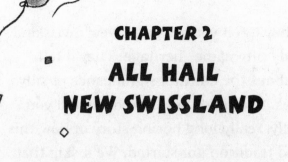

They'll tell you all about New Swissland's proud "silly name" heritage. They'll tell you about the cultural significance of silly names. And then they'll probably tell you a really, really long boring story of how this stupid tradition got started. We'll skip that part, OK?

Just remember that everybody in New Swissland has a silly name. From the richest to the poorest, from the dumbest to the smartest.

And speaking of the *smartest*, let me introduce you to Professor Pippy P. Poopypants. That's a statue of him down there in the bottom right-hand corner of the page. Now Pippy P. Poopypants was probably the smartest person in all of New Swissland. He graduated at the head of his class at Chunky Q. Boogernose University, and afterward spent all of his time creating wild and fantastic inventions.

Let's look in on him, shall we?

TiPPER Q. PPERDRiPPER

IVANA GODA de' BAFROOM

PROFESSOR PiPPY P. POOPYPANTS

Back in his private laboratory, Professor Pippy P. Poopypants was just putting the finishing touches on two wonderful new inventions: the Shrinky-Pig 2000, and the Goosy-Grow 4000.

Professor Poopypants called for his assistant, Porkbelly Funkyskunk. "Mr Funkyskunk," Pippy yelled, "I am now ready to test my new inventions!"

Porkbelly took notes while the professor aimed his Shrinky-Pig 2000 at a hideous pile of rubbish.

"BLLLLLLZZZZRRRRK!"

A powerful beam of energy blasted the garbage heap. Suddenly, the large pile of rubbish shrank to the size of a gumball.

"Hooray! It works!" cried Professor Poopypants. "Now I must try the Goosy-Grow 4000."

Pippy and Porkbelly aimed the
Goosy-Grow 4000 at an ordinary hot
dog with mustard.

"GGGGLLUUZZZZZZZZRRRRRT!"
went another bright beam of energy.

Suddenly, the hot dog grew and grew until it crashed through the walls of the laboratory.

"We did it!" exclaimed Porkbelly.

"What do you mean, *WE*?!!?" yelled Professor Poopypants. "*I* did it! *I'm* the GENIUS! You're just a lowly assistant — and don't you forget it!"

"Sorry, boss," said Porkbelly.

"With these two inventions," exclaimed Professor Poopypants, "I will be able to solve the world's rubbish problem AND create enough food for everyone on the entire planet!"

Finally, it looked as if all of the Earth's dilemmas would be fixed for ever. But who would have believed that in just a few short weeks, Professor Poopypants would be trying to take over the planet in a fit of frenzied rage?

Well, dear readers, the tragic tale is about to unfold. But before I can tell you that story, I have to tell you *this* story.

CHAPTER 3

THE FIELD TRIP

Jerome Horwitz Elementary School was having its big annual field trip to Piqua Pizza Palace. All of the kids had brought their permission slips and were lined up to get on the bus. George and Harold could hardly wait to eat pizza and play video games all afternoon.

"This is gonna RULE!" said George.

"Yeah, if we ever get there," said Harold.

"Hey," said George, "let's change the letters around on the school sign while we're waiting."

"Good idea," said Harold.

JEROME HORWITZ ELEMENTARY

PIZZA PALACE
FIELD TRIPS
ARE TODAY

So George and Harold ran over to the
sign and began their, um, *thoughtfulness*.
Unfortunately, the boys didn't notice a dark,
foreboding presence lurking nearby in the
bushes.

"A-HA!" cried Mr Krupp. "I caught you boys *red-handed*!"

"Uh-oh!" said George.

"Heh-heh," laughed Harold. "Th-this is just a little joke."

"A *JOKE*?!!?" yelled Mr Krupp. "Do you boys think that's funny???"

George and Harold thought for a moment. "Well … *yeah*," said George.

"Don't *you*?" asked Harold.

"*NO*, I don't think it's funny!" yelled Mr Krupp. "I think it's rude and offensive!"

"That's why it's funny," said George.

"*Oh*," said Mr Krupp. "You boys like to laugh, huh? Well, here's a good one: you two are officially *BANNED* from the school field trip! Instead of eating pizza, you'll spend the afternoon cleaning up the teachers' lounge! Isn't *that* funny?!!?"

"No way!" said Harold.

"That's not funny at all," said George. "That's cruel and unusual punishment."

"*That's why it's funny!*" Mr Krupp snarled.

CHAPTER 4
LEFT BEHIND

Mr Krupp marched George and Harold over to the janitor's closet.

"You can use these supplies to clean the teachers' lounge," said Mr Krupp. "I want it SPOTLESS by the time we get back!"

Mr Krupp went back outside, climbed
on to the school bus, and laughed loudly
as the buses pulled away. The teachers
all pointed at George and Harold and
laughed too.

"Rats!" said Harold. "I thought we
were going to have *fun* today!"

"We can still have fun," said George. "All we need is this ladder, that bag of powdered paste, and those big boxes of styrofoam wormy thingies."

So George and Harold carried their supplies to the teachers' lounge and got down to business.

At the sink, George pulled the sprayer nozzle, while Harold carefully taped the sprayer handle in the "on" position.

Then the two boys put the nozzle back, making sure the sprayer head was pointed in the right direction.

Next, George held the ladder steady
while Harold climbed up to the ceiling
fan. There he began scooping generous
amounts of powdered paste on to the
tops of the fan blades.

"Is this right?" asked Harold.

"Yeah," said George. "Try to get most
of it on the *ends* of the blades."

"Got it," said Harold.

209

George closed all the blinds while Harold
adjusted the ceiling fan so it would turn on
when the lights came on. Finally, the boys
filled the refrigerator up with worm-shaped
styrofoam packaging pellets.

"This is going to be *fun*," said Harold.

"Not for the teachers!" laughed George.

CHAPTER 5

THE FUN BEGINS

An hour or so later, the buses returned to the school. All of the children got off, packed up their stuff, and got ready to go home.

Mr Fyde, the science teacher, was on school bus duty. The rest of the teachers gathered around George and Harold and began teasing them.

"You kids sure did miss a *FUN* field trip!" said Ms Ribble. "The pizza was *SO* delicious! Too bad *you* didn't get any!"

"I wanted to bring you back a pizza," said Mr Meaner, "but I ate it on the bus!" He threw an empty pizza box at George and Harold's feet, and the teachers howled with laughter.

"Maybe you can lick the cheese off the box," Mr Krupp roared.

The teachers eventually got tired of taunting George and Harold, so they retreated to the teachers' lounge to relax.

"Hey, how come it's so dark in here?" asked Mr Meaner, as he flicked on the lights. The ceiling fan began rotating very slowly...

Ms Ribble went to the sink and turned
on the tap. Suddenly, the spray nozzle
sprayed cold water all over her.

"AAAAUGH!" she screamed. "Somebody
turn the water off!" The other teachers
sprang up and tried to help. They all got
sprayed, too.

The ceiling fan was rotating faster now,
and some of the powdered paste had begun
flying off the fan blades.

The teachers struggled with the tap,
pushing and shoving each other. Finally,
somebody turned the water off ... but not
before everyone was thoroughly *SOAKED*!

The ceiling fan was now spinning at full speed. All of the powder on the fan blades had been flung off, and it was now floating down on to the wet teachers.

"Hey, what the—" cried Mr Meaner.

"What's all this sticky stuff?!!?" yelled Miss Anthrope.

By now, all of the teachers were covered
in gooey, sticky paste. It didn't take a
genius to know that George and Harold
were behind all this.

"Those brats had better not have
touched my diet cola," Ms Ribble shouted.
She dashed to the refrigerator and swung
the door open.

Suddenly, thousands of tiny styrofoam
pellets flew out into the room. The wind
from the ceiling fan blew the pellets around
and around.

Naturally, they landed on the stickiest
things in the room: *the teachers*!

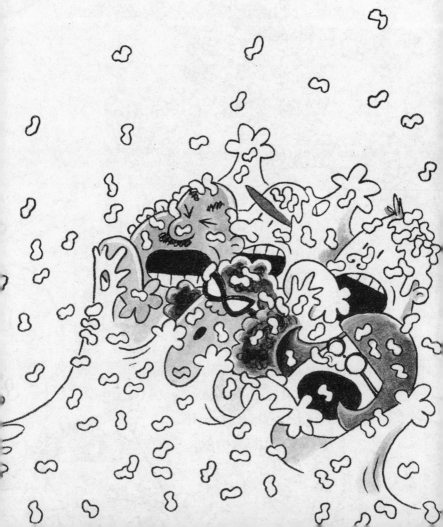

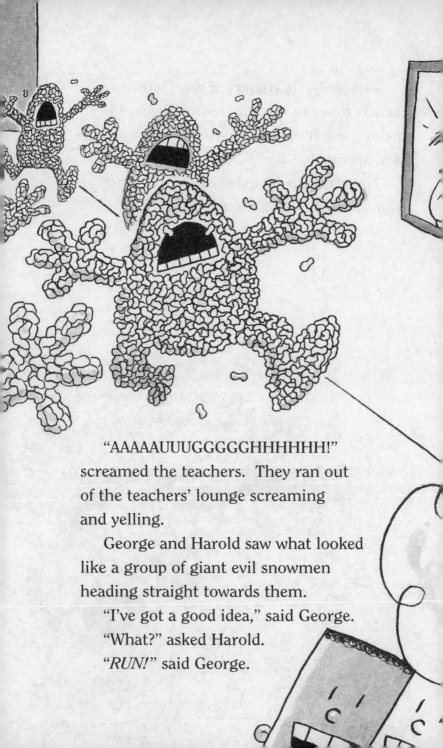

"AAAAAUUUGGGGGHHHHHH!"
screamed the teachers. They ran out
of the teachers' lounge screaming
and yelling.

George and Harold saw what looked
like a group of giant evil snowmen
heading straight towards them.

"I've got a good idea," said George.

"What?" asked Harold.

"*RUN!*" said George.

CHAPTER 6
BYE BYE, MR FYDE

The next day, George and Harold's science teacher, Mr Fyde, knocked on Mr Krupp's door.

"What do you want?" barked Mr Krupp.

"I've – I've come to resign," said Mr Fyde. "I – I just can't take it any more."

"Now hold on, pal," said Mr Krupp. "Being a teacher is hard work! You can't just quit your job when things aren't—"

"You don't understand," said Mr Fyde. "I think I'm cracking up!"

"What do you mean?" asked Mr Krupp.

"Well," said Mr Fyde. "It all started a few months ago when I had this dream that I got eaten up by a talking toilet. Then I started hearing cats and dogs meowing and growling in the classroom. Then, I imagined that the school got flooded with sticky green goop ... and just yesterday, I thought I saw a group of abominable snowmen chasing two boys down the hallway."

"Now wait just a minute, Morty," said Mr Krupp. "All of that can be explained."

"– And a few days ago," said Mr Fyde, "I thought I saw a big fat bald guy in his underwear fly out the window."

"Holy *cow*!" said Mr. Krupp. "You *ARE* crazy!"

So Mr Fyde handed in his resignation, and left Jerome Horwitz Elementary School for the greener pastures of *The Piqua Valley Home for the Reality-Challenged*.

"Now, where am I going to find a new science teacher on such short notice?" said Mr Krupp. "Where, oh where?"

CHAPTER 7

HERE, OH HERE

Remember that Poopypants guy I was telling you about back in Chapter 2? Well, things hadn't been going too well for him in the past several weeks.

Professor Poopypants had come to America to share the Shrinky-Pig 2000 and the Goosy-Grow 4000 with the world. But nobody seemed to want to hear about his inventions. They were all too busy...

…laughing at his silly name.

Poor Pippy Poopypants had been laughed out of every major scientific institution in the U.S. He'd been giggled out of Georgetown, howled out of Harvard, yuk-yukked out of Yale, snickered out of Stanford, and chuckled out of Chattanooga State Technical Community College.

Professor Poopypants was running out of money, and there was no place left for him to turn. Then, one day, the professor walked into a New York coffee shop and picked up a newspaper. And like a message from heaven, Pippy P. Poopypants found his answer.

"THAT'S IT!" he cried. "I'll become an elementary school science teacher!"

"I'll work really hard, and soon, people will come to respect me and see what a genius I am. *Then* I can introduce my great inventions to the world!"

Pippy Poopypants was certain that the one place people *wouldn't* laugh at his name was at an elementary school. "Kids are so accepting and loving," he said. "You can always count on the sweetness and innocence of children!"

226

CHAPTER 8

THE SWEETNESS AND INNOCENCE OF CHILDREN

"Hello, boys and girls," said the professor a week later. "I'm going to be your new science teacher. My name is…

…Professor Pippy P. Poopypants."

"All right, settle down, boys and girls. Yes, yes, it's a funny name, I know, but let me explain how I got this name. Please, children, settle down. It's not that funny, let me assure you. Um … boys and girls … BOYS AND GIRLS! Please stop laughing! All right, I'm going to count to ten, and when I'm done, I want all of you to quiet down so we can learn about the wonderful world of science. One, two, three, four, five, six, seven … eight … nine … nine

and a half ... ummm. Children, PLEASE
STOP LAUGHING! I know you're all very
far behind in your lessons, and we've got
a lot of catching up to do. Boys and girls!
STOP IT! I'm not going to tell you again!
IT'S NOT FUNNY! There's no reason at
all for you to be laughing at my name!
I'm sure we *all* have funny names if you
think about it. STOP IT RIGHT NOW! OK,
boys and girls, I'll just wait until you all
settle down. I can wait..."

A week later, things hadn't got any
better. Professor Poopypants was really
beginning to get angry.

"How am I going to get through to these
children?" he asked himself. "Hey! I've got
it! I'll create a wonderful new invention!"

CHAPTER 9
THE GERBIL JOGGER 2000

The next morning, Professor Poopypants came to school with an odd-looking miniature robot.

"Look, children," he said. "I've created a new invention using the principles of science! I call it the Gerbil Jogger 2000."

The children stopped laughing for a moment and looked with interest at Professor Poopypants's new invention.

"You see, children," said the professor, "some people like to jog, and their pets like to jog along beside them. That's fine if you have a dog or a cat, but what if you have a pet gerbil? It used to be a big problem, but not any more!"

Professor Poopypants opened the glass dome on the Gerbil Jogger 2000 and inserted a cute, fuzzy gerbil.

The gerbil pushed his tiny legs against the simple controls, and suddenly the machine came to life. In no time at all, the gerbil was jogging around the classroom in his robot suit. The children were delighted!

"Wow!" said Connor Mancini. "Science is COOL!" All of the other children agreed.

"This is wonderful!" thought Professor Poopypants. "I've REACHED them! Now I can *TEACH* them!"

"Um, excuse me," said George to the professor. "What's your *middle* name?"

"My middle name," said the professor proudly, "is *Pee-Pee*. Why do you ask?"

At that point, the children picked up where they had left off: laughing at Professor Pippy *Pee-Pee* Poopypants's ridiculous name.

The professor began to shake with anger. Tiny veins in his forehead started growing, and his face turned bright red. "I can't take much more of this," the furious professor said through clenched teeth. "I think I might blow a fuse if *just one more thing* happens!"

CHAPTER 10
JUST ONE MORE THING

Soon afterwards, in reading class, the children all heard the story of the Pied Piper of Hamelin.

"You know," said George, "that story gives me an idea!"

So George and Harold began working on their newest comic book: *Captain Underpants and the Pied Pooper of Piqua*.

That afternoon, they sneaked into the office and ran off copies of their new adventure to sell in the playground. And everything would have been just fine if one of the third graders hadn't left his copy lying around in the hallway.

CAPTAIN UNDERPANTS
And The Pied Pooper of Piqua

Story By George Beard • Pictures by Harold Hutchins

Onse Upon a time in the city of Piqua, OHIO, there was A sciense Teacher Whose name was Pippy PoopyPants

my middel name is Pee - Pee.

Everybody Laffed at his funny name.

HA HA HA HA!

This made Pippy MAD!

I'LL Show them!

So He BiLT An Army of Girble Jogger Two Thousands.

HAHA

PP PP PP PP

He put a Girbles in each one

Hey, MAN!

But He couldent make Them do Any EViL Stuff.

RATS!

TAP TAP

Then he thought of a evil plan!

But of corse!

He made A bunch of Little Headphones And put Them on the gerbils.

Hey

Soon, Professor poopypantses Army OF GirbEL JOGGER TWO Thousands Were off on a evil RAMPAGE.

They ALL HEAded straight for the School!

HAHAHAHAH

Help! The Girble Jogger TWO thousands broke in The Caffateria. They Just Knocked over some cupcakes and now There Attacking the gym teacher!

Quick--- Somebody SAve the CUPCAKES!

Professer Poopypants and his evil Army Rounded up all The children.

Follow me! HA HA HA

This Looks Like A JOB for...

CAPTAIN UNDERPANTS!

what seems to Be the problem?

I'm TAKing These kids To be my sLaves

And just who Do You Think You Are?

I'm Professer Poopypants

HA HA HA HA HA HA HA HA HA HA HA HA HA HA HA HA HA HA HA HA

Professor Poopypants WAS really mad. So He pressed A Button on his bowtie...

 click

HA HA HA

...And His Bowtie Transformed him...

 CHK- CHK-

...into...

 CHUCKA CHUCKA

...A...

 Foosh Foosh

...GiAnt...

KA-CHUNK KA-CHUNK

...CYBORG!!!

HA HA HA HA

UH OH!

They had A big Fight!

BUT CAPTAIN UNDERPANTS WAS faster Than A speeding WAISTbAnd....

 zip

...MORE POWERFUL Than Boxer Shorts...

OWIE!

...And Abel To leap tall buildings without getting a wedgie!

TRA-LA-LAAA!

Professor Poopypants chased our hero to a car scrapyard.

I've got you Now, Waistband Warrior!

KLUNK

Now I'm gunna crush You!

OFF
START

BIG CRUSHER Thingy 2000

Captain Underpants pressed a button on his "Utility Waistband"

CLICK!

And out popped the Tiny Toilet of Truth.

CLICK

Captain Underpants Aimed the Tiny Toilet of Truth at Robo-Pippy.

B
C
T
2

NOTISE: ALL ANIMAL cruelty WAS SIMULATED. No ActuAL Girbles were Forsed To listen to CHer.
Treehouse Comix

CHAPTER 12

PROFESSOR P. GOES CRA-Z

In his entire life, Professor Poopypants had never been as angry as he was at that very moment. As he stood in the hallway, something inside his fragile brain snapped. He began shaking and sweating uncontrollably.

Suddenly, a wicked smile stretched across the professor's face. He staggered toward his empty classroom, mumbling to himself and giggling. He had hit rock bottom, and he decided to pull the rest of the planet down with him. Pippy P. Poopypants was going to take over the world!

But before I can tell you that story, I have to tell you ... oh, never mind. I'll just tell you that story.

CHAPTER 13

HONEY, I SHRUNK THE SCHOOL

Professor Poopypants opened the storage cupboard in his classroom and took out the Shrinky-Pig 2000 and the Goosy-Grow 4000. He also grabbed the empty Gerbil Jogger 2000, and stumbled outside with his inventions.

The crazed professor giggled wildly to himself as he aimed the Goosy-Grow 4000 at the Gerbil Jogger 2000.

"GGGGLLUUZZZZZZZRRRRRT!"

Suddenly, the Gerbil Jogger 2000 grew
ten storeys high.

Professor Poopypants began his long
climb up the side of the giant Gerbil Jogger
2000. It took almost an hour, but eventually
he reached the huge glass dome at the top
and squeezed his way inside.

"Mummy?" said a little boy who was walking by with his mother. "A little old man just crawled into a giant robot suit and is about to take over a school!"

"Oh, for heaven's sake!" said his mother. "Where do you come up with this nonsense?!!? Next you'll be telling me that a giant man in his underwear is fighting the huge robot in the middle of the city!"

Professor Poopypants was now in control of the colossal Gerbil Jogger 2000. He reached down with its mighty arm, picked up the Shrinky-Pig 2000, and aimed it at the school.

"BLLLLLLZZZZRRRRK!"

Just then, George and Harold looked out
the window. "Hey," said George, "isn't that
the gerbil robot thingy?"

"Yeah," said Harold. "Why is it so big?"

"I don't know," said George, "but it's
getting bigger by the second!"

"Um..." said Harold, "I don't think it's getting bigger ... I think *WE'RE* getting *smaller*!"

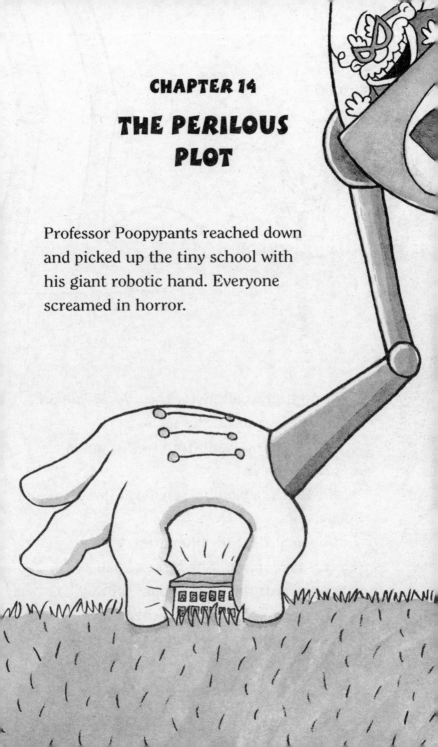

CHAPTER 14

THE PERILOUS PLOT

Professor Poopypants reached down and picked up the tiny school with his giant robotic hand. Everyone screamed in horror.

In no time at all, Eyewitness Newswoman
Ingrid Ashley was on the scene.

"What do you want from us?" shouted
reporter Ashley.

"I want … a *pencil*!" screamed Professor
Poopypants.

"A pencil?!!?" asked Reporter Ashley.
"Here – take mine." She tossed a yellow
pencil towards the giant robot.

Professor Poopypants reached down with
his giant robot arm, picked up the Goosy-
Grow 4000, and aimed it at the pencil.

"GGGGLLUUZZZZZZZZRRRRRT!"

The pencil grew to the size of a tree trunk, and Professor Poopypants grabbed it.

"Follow me," he said.

The giant robot led the news crew to the centre of downtown Piqua. There, he found three large white billboards. He put down the Shrinky-Pig 2000 and the Goosy-Grow 4000, and began writing on the billboards with his giant pencil.

CHAPTER 15

THE NAME CHANGE-O-CHART 2000

Professor Poopypants spent several minutes jotting down a complex code on the three giant billboards.

George and Harold, along with nearly a thousand of their fellow shrunken students, watched the mad professor from the terrifying clutch of his giant robotic hand.

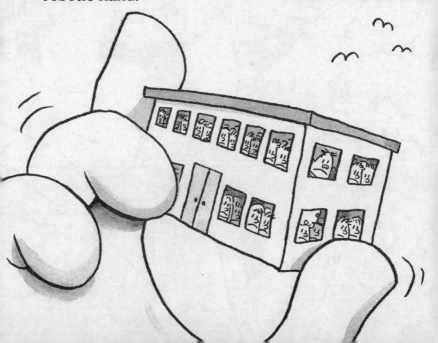

"What is that crazy guy up to?" asked Mr Krupp from his office window.

"I'LL TELL YOU," shouted Pippy Poopypants. "Everybody on the planet must now change their normal names into silly names using these three charts! Anyone who refuses will get *SHRUNK*!"

"How do the charts work?" asked Mr Krupp.

"It's easy," said Professor Poopypants. "What's your first name?"

"Er … I'm not telling," said Mr Krupp.

"*WHAT IS YOUR FIRST NAME?!!?*"
shouted Professor Poopypants.

"All right, all right," said Mr Krupp. "It's,
uh … *Benny*." All of the children giggled.

"So the first letter of your first name is
'B'," said Pippy. "Now look at the first chart
and find the letter 'B'."

1

FIRST CHART: USE the FiRST LetteR of YouR FiRSt NAME
To DeteRMine YouR **NEW** FiRST NAME!

A= STinky
B= LumpY
C= Buttercup
D= Gidget
E= CRusty
F= GReasy
G= FLuffY
H= CheeseBall
I= Chim-Chim

J= Poopsie
K= FLunky
L= Booger
M= Pinky
N= ZippY
O= GOOBER
P= DooFus
Q= SLimy

R= LOOPY
S= SnottY
T= FALAFeL
U= DoRkY
V= SqueeZit
W= OpRAH
X= SkippeR
Y= Dinky
Z= ZSA-ZSA

SECON
to de

A= [
B= '
C= C
D= B
E= G
F= B
G= L
H= W
I= C

Mr Krupp looked at the chart. "It says 'B = Lumpy'," he whined.

"Good!" said Professor Poopypants. "Your NEW first name is '*LUMPY*!'"

All of the children laughed.

"*Lumpy* Krupp?!!?" moaned Mr Krupp. "I don't want to be called 'Lumpy Krupp'."

"You won't!" laughed Professor Poopypants. "Because you have to change your *last* name, too!"

"Uh, oh," said Mr Krupp.

"Your last name is 'Krupp'," said the professor, "which starts with a 'K' and ends with a 'P'. Now find the letter 'K' on the second chart, and the letter 'P' on the third chart."

1

First Chart: Use the First Letter of Your First NAME To Determine Your NEW FIRST NAME!

A= Stinky
B= Lumpy
C= Buttercup
D= Gidget
E= Crusty
F= Greasy
G= Fluffy
H= Cheeseball
I= Chim-Chim

J= Poopsie
K= Flunky
L= Booger
M= Pinky
N= Zippy
O= Goober
P= Doofus
Q= Slimy

R= Loopy
S= Snotty
T= Falafel
U= Dorky
V= Squeezit
W= Oprah
X= Skipper
Y= Dinky
Z= Zsa-Zsa

2

Second Chart: Use the First Letter of your LAST NAME to determine the First half of your NEW LAST NAME.

A= Diaper
B= Toilet
C= Giggle
D= Bubble
E= Girdle
F= Barf
G= Lizard
H= Waffle
I= Cootie

J= Monkey
K= Potty
L= Liver
M= Banana
N= Rhino
O= Burger
P= Hamster
Q= Toad

R= Gizzard
S= Pizza
T= Gerbil
U= Chicken
V= Pickle
W= Chuckle
X= Tofu
Y= Gorilla
Z= Stinker

Third Char To determi

A= Head
B= Mouth
C= Face
D= Nose
E= Tush
F= Breath
G= Pants
H= Shorts
I= Lips

Mr Krupp looked at the two charts.

"It says, 'K = Potty' and 'P = biscuit'."

"Wonderful!" shouted the professor. "Your new last name is 'Pottybiscuits'."

"Oh, no!" groaned the principal. "My new name is *Lumpy Pottybiscuits*!'"

The children all howled with laughter.

1

FIRST CHART: Use the First Letter of Your FIRST NAME To Determine Your NEW FIRST NAME!

A = Stinky
B = Lumpy
C = Buttercup
D = Gidget
E = Crusty
F = Greasy
G = Fluffy
H = Cheeseball
I = Chim-Chim
J = Poopsie
K = Flunky
L = Booger
M = Pinky
N = Zippy
O = Goober
P = Doofus
Q = Slimy
R = Loopy
S = Snotty
T = Falafel
U = Dorky
V = Squeezit
W = Oprah
X = Skipper
Y = Dinky
Z = Zsa-Zsa

2

SECOND CHART: USE the first Letter of your LAST Name to determine the first half of your NEW Last Name.

A = Diaper
B = Toilet
C = Giggle
D = Bubble
E = Girdle
F = Barf
G = Lizard
H = Waffle
I = Cootie
J = Monkey
K = Potty
L = Liver
M = Banana
N = Rhino
O = Burger
P = Hamster
Q = Toad
R = Gizzard
S = Pizza
T = Gerbil
U = Chicken
V = Pickle
W = Chuckle
X = Tofu
Y = Gorilla
Z = Stinker

"Don't laugh *too* hard, kiddies," said Professor Poopypants. "You all have to change your names, too, or I'll shrink you again!"

Well, as you can imagine, nobody wanted to get shrunk *twice*! So everybody looked at the three charts and figured out their new, silly names.

3

Third Chart: Use The Last Letter of your Last Name To determine the Second half of your **NEW** Last Name.

A = Head
B = Mouth
C = Face
D = Nose
E = Tush
F = Breath
G = Pants
H = Shorts
I = Lips
J = Honker
K = Butt
L = Brain
M = Tushie
N = Chunks
O = Hiney
P = Biscuits
Q = Toes
R = Buns
S = Fanny
T = Sniffer
U = Sprinkles
V = Kisser
W = Squirt
X = Humperdinck
Y = Brains
Z = Juice

Stephanie Yarkoff became "Snotty Gorillabreath". Robbie Staenberg became "Loopy Pizzapants", and poor little Janet Warwick became "Poopsie Chucklebutt".

"This may be the most horrible moment in all of human history," said the local news reporter to her audience. "It seems that everyone on Earth must now change his or her name to avoid getting shrunk! Good luck to you all!

"This is Chim-Chim Diaperbrains reporting for Eyewitness News. Now, back to you, Booger."

266

CHAPTER 16

FLUFFY AND CHEESEBALL

This is Fluffy Toiletnose and Cheeseball
Wafflefanny. Fluffy is the kid on the left
with the tie and the flat-top. Cheeseball is
the one on the right with the T-shirt and
the bad haircut. Remember that now.

"We've got to do something," cried Fluffy.

"But what?" said Cheeseball. "We're smaller than two mice … what could we possibly do?"

"Let's go find our old friend, Captain Underpants!" said Fluffy.

So Fluffy and Cheeseball ran to Mr Pottybiscuits's office and found him cowering under his desk.

"I can't believe I'm about to do this," said Fluffy, "but here goes nothing!"

Fluffy snapped his fingers.

"SNAP!"

Suddenly, a strange change came over
Lumpy Pottybiscuits. His worried frown
quickly turned into a heroic smile. He
rose from behind his desk and thrust out
his chest.

In no time at all, Mr Pottybiscuits had removed his outer clothing and tied a red curtain around his neck.

"Tra-La-LAAAA!" sang the hero. "Captain Underpants is here!"

"Cool!" said Cheeseball. "But from now on you have to call yourself 'Buttercup Chickenfanny'. The guy in the gerbil suit says so!"

"Hey," said Captain Underpants, "I don't take orders from *ANYBODY*!"

"Great," said Fluffy. "Now fly out that window and bring back that big machine thingy with the Lava Lamp on top."

"Yes, *SIR*," said Captain Underpants.

CHAPTER 17

CAPTAIN UNDERPANTS TO THE RESCUE

Captain Underpants flew down to the ground and grabbed the Goosy-Grow 4000. But on his way back up, he was spotted by Professor Poopypants.

The evil professor zapped Captain Underpants with a bolt of energy from the Shrinky-Pig 2000.

"BLLLLLLZZZZRRRRK!"

Suddenly, the Waistband Warrior began
to shrink even *smaller* than before. He flew
back to the tiny school carrying an
extremely small Goosy-Grow 4000, and he
dropped it into Fluffy's hand.

"Hey, where's Captain Underpants?"
asked Fluffy.

"I don't know," said Cheeseball. "I think
he got shrunk so small that we can't see
him any more."

"Well," said Fluffy, "at least we have this little invention thingy."

"How's that going to help us?" asked Cheeseball.

"I saw Professor Poopypants use it to make that pencil grow really big," said Fluffy. "It's our only hope of ever getting back to normal size!"

"I hope it still works," said Cheeseball.

Fluffy and Cheeseball dashed to the
school kitchen and climbed up the ladder
on to the roof.

"Maybe if we zap the school with this
thing, everybody will grow back to normal
size," said Fluffy.

"Good idea," said Cheeseball. "Then we
can all run away!"

CHAPTER 18

ARE YOU THERE, GOD? IT'S US, FLUFFY AND CHEESEBALL

Fluffy pointed the Goosy-Grow 4000 at the roof of the school and got ready to press the button. But the boys were spotted by Professor Poopypants. Quickly, he turned his mighty robotic hand, and Fluffy and Cheeseball slid off the roof. Downward they tumbled through the air.

"Oh NO," shouted Cheeseball. "We're DOOMED!"

"Wait a second," cried Fluffy. "Do you have a piece of paper on you?"

"Yeah," screamed Cheeseball. "Right here in my pocket. But what good is it gonna do us now?"

"Quick!" cried Fluffy. "Fold it into a paper aeroplane!"

"What *kind* of paper aeroplane?" asked Cheeseball.

"*ANY KIND!*" screamed Fluffy. "JUST DO IT NOW!"

Quickly, Cheeseball folded the paper into a goofy-looking glider. "How's this?" he screamed.

"Great!" yelled Fluffy. "Now hold it steady!" Fluffy pointed the tiny Goosy-Grow 4000 at Cheeseball's aeroplane, and he pressed the button.

"GGGGLLUUZZZZZZZZRRRRRT!"

Suddenly, Cheeseball's aeroplane grew
to an enormous size. Fluffy and Cheeseball
flopped down into it, and the paper
aeroplane took off, gliding through the air.

"Oh, MAN!" cried Cheeseball. "I can't
believe that worked!"

"We're not out of this yet!" yelled Fluffy.

CHAPTER 19

THE FLIGHT OF THE GOOFY GLIDER

Fluffy and Cheeseball had to admit that it was pretty cool flying over the city streets on a paper aeroplane. They didn't even seem to mind the fact that they were only about two centimetres tall each.

But you can probably imagine the boys' concern when they started heading straight for a wood chipper.

"Oh, NO!" cried Fluffy. "We're gonna get, um ... *WOOD CHIPPERED* to death!"

Cheeseball couldn't look. He put his hands over his eyes and waited for the inevitable.

But suddenly, *SWOOOOSH!* The paper aeroplane swerved sharply and missed the wood chipper altogether.

"Hey!" cried Fluffy. "How did that happen?"

"I don't know," said Cheeseball. "*I'm* not steering this thing!"

The boys had barely caught their breath
when a small dog noticed the aeroplane and
came running after them.

"Oh, NO!" cried Cheeseball. "We're
gonna get eaten by a *SAUSAGE DOG*!"

Fluffy covered *his* eyes this time.

But wouldn't you know it, the aeroplane swerved sharply upward and out of the range of the little dog altogether.

"Are you doing that?" asked Cheeseball.

"No," said Fluffy. "It must be the wind!"

Finally, the paper aeroplane landed in a wet, sticky pile of hot tar.

"Yuck!" said Fluffy. "What could be worse than gettin' stuck in a pile of *tar*?"

"Maybe getting crushed by a big steamroller thingy," said Cheeseball.

"You sure have an active imagination," said Fluffy.

"No, I don't," said Cheeseball, as he pointed upward. "*Look!*"

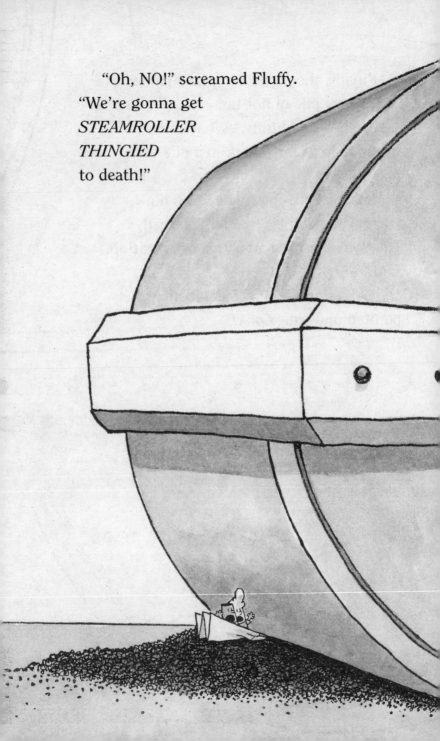

Just then, the boys were yanked up by the backs of their shirts and carried off through the air to safety.

"Something's got hold of us!" cried Cheeseball. "But I can't see what it is!"

"It must be Captain Underpants," said Fluffy. "We just can't see him because he's so small!"

"Hey," said Cheeseball, "I'll bet he was steering the aeroplane out of danger, too!"

"*OUR HERO!*" the boys shouted.

CHAPTER 20

X-TRA, X-TRA, X-TRA, X-TRA, X-TRA, X-TRA, X-TRA, X-TRA, X-TRA LARGE UNDERPANTS

Fluffy and Cheeseball landed safely in an abandoned alley.

"We've got to enlarge Captain Underpants so he can fight Professor Poopypants," said Fluffy. "The fate of the entire planet is in our hands!"

"But how can we enlarge him if we can't even see him?" asked Cheeseball.

"Good question," said Fluffy.

"Wait," said Cheeseball. "I've got an idea." He called out as loud as he could: "Captain Underpants! We can't see you, but if you can hear us, fly over and land on my finger. We have a machine that can make you big again."

The boys waited a few seconds.

"Look, Fluffy!" said Cheeseball. "There he is! See? He's that little tiny speck on my finger. Now just aim the machine at that little speck ... but don't zap my finger, OK?"

"Don't worry," said Fluffy. "I'm a great shot with this thing. I won't zap your..."

"GGGGLLUUZZZZZZZZRRRRRT!"

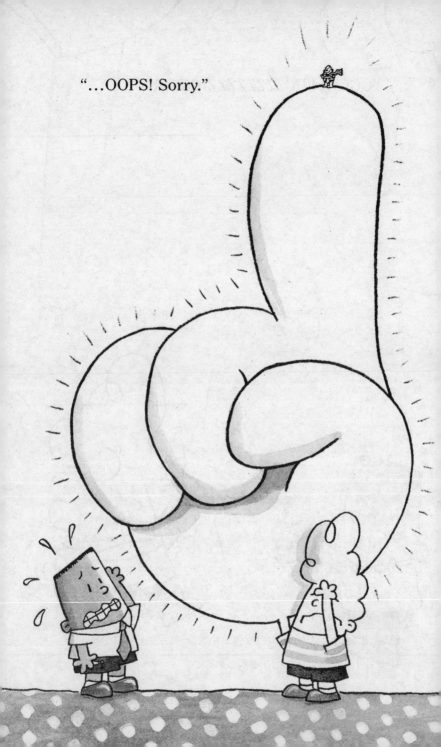

The good news was that Captain
Underpants had grown larger and was now
visible. The bad news was, well, let's just say
that Cheeseball was going to have an awful
hard time picking his nose with his right
hand from now on.

Fluffy gave Captain Underpants a few
more shots from the Goosy-Grow 4000. The
Waistband Warrior grew and grew and grew
until he was ten storeys high.

Finally, the colossal captain headed
towards the preposterous professor. A
showdown was about to begin.

The little boy from Chapter 13 happened
to be walking by with his mother again.
He looked up and saw a giant man in his
underwear getting ready to fight a huge
robot in the middle of the city.

"Mummy?" said the little boy.

"What?" asked his mother.

"Umm ... never mind," said the boy.

CHAPTER 21

THE INCREDIBLY GRAPHIC VIOLENCE CHAPTER (IN FLIP-O-RAMA™)

WARNING:

The following chapter contains scenes that are so intense and horrific, they may not be suitable for viewing by people who can't take a joke.

If you are easily offended, or if you tend to blame all of society's evils on TV shows and cartoon characters, please run to your nearest supermarket and get a life. They're located in the "Get Real" section next to the clues.

Good luck!

PILKEY® BRAND
D-RAMA

HERE'S HOW IT WORKS!

STEP 1
Place your *left* hand inside the dotted lines marked "LEFT HAND HERE". Hold the book open *flat*.

STEP 2
Grasp the *right-hand* page with your right thumb and index finger (inside the dotted lines marked "RIGHT THUMB HERE").

STEP 3
Now *quickly* flip the right-hand page back and forth until the picture appears to be *animated*.

(For extra fun, try adding your own sound-effects!)

FLIP-O-RAMA 1

(pages 297 and 299)

Remember, flip *only* page 297.
While you are flipping, be sure you
can see the picture on page 297
and the one on page 299.
If you flip quickly, the two
pictures will start to look like
<u>one</u> *animated* picture.

Don't forget to
add your own sound-effects!

LEFT HAND HERE

PROFESSOR POOPYPANTS PACKED A POWERFUL PUNCH!

RIGHT
THUMB
HERE

RIGHT
INDEX
FINGER
HERE

PROFESSOR POOPYPANTS PACKED A POWERFUL PUNCH!

FLIP-O-RAMA 2

(pages 301 and 303)

Remember, flip *only* page 301.
While you are flipping, be sure you
can see the picture on page 301
and the one on page 303.
If you flip quickly, the two
pictures will start to look like
<u>one</u> *animated* picture.

Don't forget to
add your own sound-effects!

LEFT HAND HERE

BUT THE HEAD-BUTTIN' HERO HALTED THE HORROR!

RIGHT
THUMB
HERE

RIGHT
INDEX
FINGER
HERE

BUT THE HEAD-BUTTIN' HERO HALTED THE HORROR!

FLIP-O-RAMA 3

(pages 305 and 307)

Remember, flip *only* page 305.
While you are flipping, be sure you
can see the picture on page 305
and the one on page 307.
If you flip quickly, the two
pictures will start to look like
<u>one</u> *animated* picture.

Don't forget to
add your own sound-effects!

LEFT HAND HERE

THE BRIEF-WEARIN' BANDIT BATTLED THE BIONIC BEHEMOTH!

305

RIGHT THUMB HERE

RIGHT
INDEX
FINGER
HERE

THE BRIEF-WEARIN'
BANDIT BATTLED THE
BIONIC BEHEMOTH!

FLIP-O-RAMA 4

(pages 309 and 311)

Remember, flip *only* page 309.
While you are flipping, be sure you
can see the picture on page 309
and the one on page 311.
If you flip quickly, the two
pictures will start to look like
<u>one</u> *animated* picture.

Don't forget to
add your own sound-effects!

LEFT HAND HERE

THE WAISTBAND
WARRIOR WON
THE WAR!

309

RIGHT
THUMB
HERE

RIGHT
INDEX
FINGER
HERE

310

THE WAISTBAND
WARRIOR WON
THE WAR!

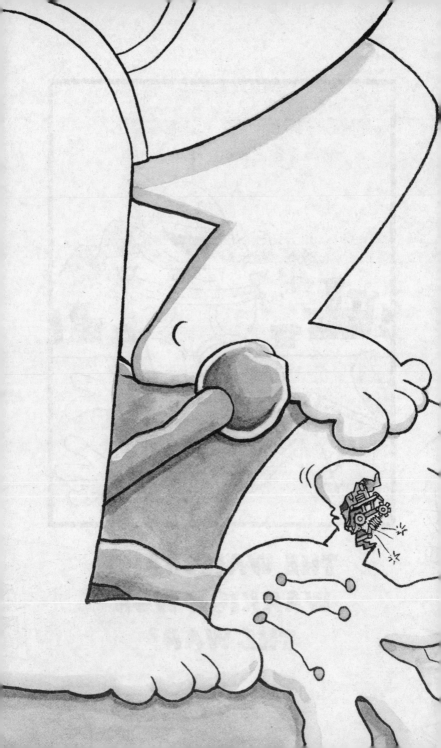

CHAPTER 22

THE TWENTY-SECOND CHAPTER

Professor Poopypants had been defeated, and everybody in the school cheered wildly. They were still small, but at least they got their old names back.

"I'm so glad I don't have a silly name any more," said Ms Ribble.

"Me, too," said Mr Rected.

"Hooray!" cried George. "Let's all give Captain Underpants a big *hand*!"

Harold was not amused.

"Oops…" said George. "Sorry."

"That's OK," said Harold. "Just gimme that invention thing so I can zap us back to normal!"

TAP
TAP
TAP

Harold held the Goosy-Grow 4000 in his
giant hand and zapped George and himself
(that is, every part of himself *EXCEPT* his
giant hand).

"GGGGLLUUZZZZZZZRRRRRT!"

Suddenly, George and Harold were back to their normal sizes again.

"Boy," said George, "we sure have tested the limits of science today!"

"Yep!" said Harold, "*and* the limits of our readers' willing suspension of disbelief!"

"Er ... *yyyeah*," said George, "that, too!"

George and Harold picked up their tiny school and carried it back to where it belonged. George got ready to zap the school with the Goosy-Grow 4000, while Harold prepared to zap Captain Underpants with the Shrinky-Pig 2000.

"I sure hope this works," said George.

"Me, too," said Harold.

CHAPTER 23

TO MAKE A LONG STORY SHORT

It did.

CHAPTER 24

THE CHAPTER BEFORE THE LAST CHAPTER

George took Captain Underpants over to the bushes behind the school and ordered him to dress back up like Mr Krupp.

"Let's go, pal," said George. "We haven't got all day!"

Then Harold had some fun with the garden hose. In no time at all, Mr Krupp was back to his old nasty self again.

Soon the cops showed up to arrest Professor Poopypants.

"There's one thing I don't understand," said George to the professor. "Wouldn't it have been *smarter* to change *your own name* instead of forcing the rest of the world to change theirs?"

"Gosh," said Professor Poopypants, "I never thought of that!"

A few weeks later, George and Harold received a letter from the Piqua State Penitentiary.

Dear George and Harold,

Sorry about trying to overthrow the world and everything. I've decided to take your advice and change my name so that people won't laugh at me anymore.

From now on I'll be going by my Grandfather's name (on my mother's side). It's such a relief knowing that nobody will ever make fun of my name again.

Signed,
Tippy Tinkletrousers

CHAPTER 25

THE CHAPTER AFTER THE CHAPTER BEFORE THE LAST CHAPTER

"You know," said George, "I really learned something today."

"What's that?" asked Harold.

"I learned that it's not nice to make fun of people," said George.

"Wow," said Harold. "I think this is the first time one of our stories ever had a *moral*!"

"Probably the last time, too," said George.

"Let's hope so," said Harold.

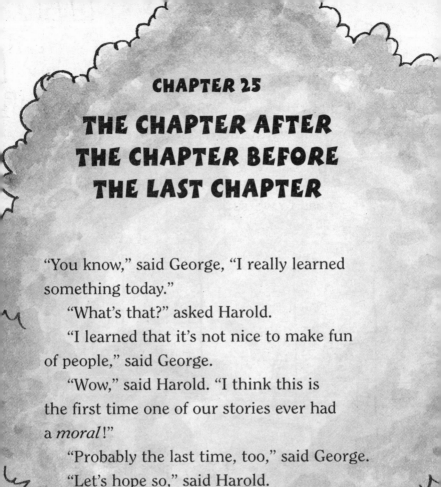

But George and Harold had forgotten all about the *other* moral they had learned along the way, which was: "Don't ever, ever, *EVER* hypnotize your principal."

Because if you do, your life can go from bad to worse...

...at the *snap* of a finger!

"OH, NO!" screamed Harold.

"HERE WE GO AGAIN!" screamed
George.

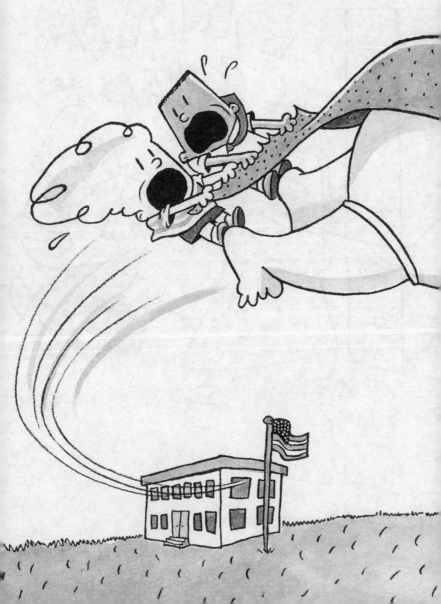

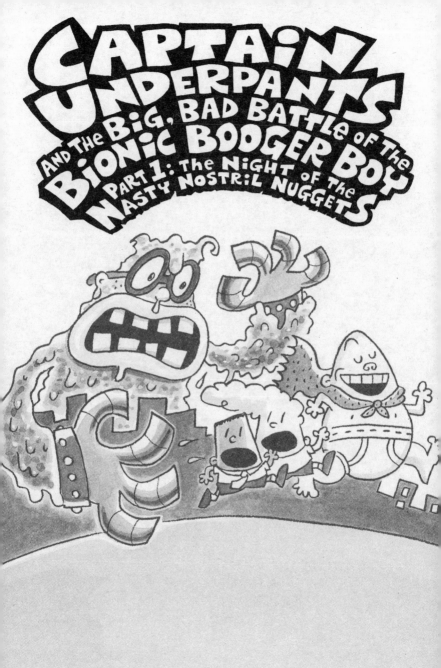

FOR AMY AND JODI

CHAPTERS

George and Harold Prowdly Present

THE AWFUL Truth ABOut CAPTAIN UNDERPANts

A Treehouse Comix PRoDuction

Onse upon a time there was two cool Kids named George and Harold.

We Da man! / me too.

They had a mean old Prin-sipel named Mr Krupp.

GRRRR / Hey Bubs! / Blah Blah Blah

One time Mr Krupp Punished George and Harold.

You half To OBey my orders

So they got a 3-D Hypno Ring and Hypnotised him.

No way! you must obey us now / ok.

Then one day he got atacked by a dandyLion.

Dont you hate it when that happens?

Help.

So George stole Some Super Power Juice From a U.F.O.

Ouchy!

S.P.J.

and gave it to him.

Down the hach!

Glug
Glug
Glug

S.P.J.

Sudenly, he got Super Powers.

Hey I can Fly now. I RULE!

OH Great.

Bummer

Nowadays, whenever Mr Krupp hears anybody snap there fingers...

Snap

... He turns into you-know-who!

Tra-La-Laaaa!

UH OH

NOT again

And the only way you can stop him is if you pore water on his head.

H2O

what the?

Then he turns back into Mr Krupp.

Hey whats the big idea bubs?

So whatever you do, Dont snap your fingers around Mr Krupp ok?

CHAPTER 1
GEORGE AND HAROLD

This is George Beard and Harold Hutchins.
George is the kid on the left with the tie
and the flat-top. Harold is the one on the
right with the T-shirt and the bad haircut.
Remember that now.

George's and Harold's grades in school were much like whales in the ocean: They rarely rose above "C" level.

Melvin Sneedly, however (he's the kid down there with the bow tie and the glasses), always got straight A's.

Because Melvin was so academically gifted, people just assumed he was a lot smarter than George and Harold.

But that wasn't true.

You see, George and Harold were every bit as smart as the *straight A* students . . . but in a *different* way. In a way that couldn't be measured by quizzes or worksheets.

Maybe George and Harold couldn't spell very well or remember their multiplication tables. Perhaps their grammar weren't no good neither. But when it came to saving the entire planet from the nasty forces of unrelenting evil, there was nobody better than George Beard and Harold Hutchins.

It's a good thing that George and Harold were smart enough to get themselves out of trouble, because their silliness was always getting them *into* trouble. In fact, one time it got them into a really *SNOTTY* situation.

But before I can tell you that story, I have to tell you *this* story...

CHAPTER 2

SQUISHIES, PART 1

It was Demonstration Speech Day in
Ms Ribble's fourth-grade English class.
Every student had to give an oral report
demonstrating how to do something. First
up were Tim Bronski and Stevie Loopner,
who demonstrated how to give a speech
that they hadn't prepared for.

They got a D-.

Next up were Jessica Gordon and Stephanie Wycoff, who demonstrated how to cook frozen lasagne in a pop-up toaster.

After the firemen left, it was George and Harold's turn. Harold carefully tacked some charts and graphs on to the wall while George brought out a large garbage can with a toilet seat taped to the top.

SiDe Veiw

"Ladies and gentlemen," said George. "Today Harold and I are going to demonstrate how to do a 'Squishy'. First, you need two packs of ketchup and a toilet seat."

"Next," said Harold as he pointed to their display chart, "you must fold the ketchup packs in half and carefully place them under the toilet seat. Make sure that the packs are under those front two bumpy thingies on the bottom of the seat."

"Now, once the ketchup packs are in place," said Harold, "all you have to do is wait for somebody to sit down on the toilet seat. Do we have any volunteers?"

"C'mon," said George, "who wants a Squishy?"

Although nobody in the class wanted to sit on the toilet seat, everybody wanted to see what would happen if somebody actually DID. So George grasped one side of the toilet seat, Harold grasped the other, and together they pushed down.

SPLAT!!! SPLAT!!!

SPLAT

Everyone in the class was thrilled
(except for the two kids sitting directly in
front of the toilet seat, who were somewhat
less-than-thrilled). "Hooray for Squishies!"
the children shouted.

Now, normally George and Harold's
teacher, Ms Ribble, would have been very
angry about this particular demonstration
speech.

She would have yelled on and on about "imitateable behaviour" and how it's not nice to spray ketchup into people's underwear. But Ms Ribble had changed quite a bit since the last book, and now she was all about FUN!

"C'mon, kids," shouted Ms Ribble. "Let's all run to the cafeteria and grab some ketchup packs! Squishies for EVERYBODY!!!"

"HOORAY!" cried the children as they bounded from their seats and dashed towards the classroom door.

"NOT SO FAST!" shouted Melvin Sneedly, who stood blocking the door with his arms spread defiantly. "You guys are *so* immature!"

CHAPTER 3
THE COMBINE-O-TRON 2000

Melvin Sneedly, the school brainiac, was not about to let anybody leave the classroom until he had given his demonstration speech.

"We still have fifteen minutes left before lunch," said Melvin, "and that's just enough time for me to demonstrate my new invention, the Combine-O-Tron 2000."

"Aww, *maaaan!*" whined Melvin's classmates.

The children all slumped back into their seats while Melvin pushed a plastic rolling cart to the front of the classroom. On top of the cart were a hamster, a small robot (which Melvin had built himself), and a strange-looking contraption shaped like an ice-cream cone.

"Today," said Melvin, "I will demonstrate how to turn an ordinary hamster into your very own bionic cyber-slave."

Melvin placed his pet hamster, Sulu, at one end of the cart, and his tiny homemade robot at the other end. "I shall now combine this ordinary hamster with this tiny robot using the Combine-O-Tron 2000."

Melvin picked up the Combine-O-Tron 2000 and turned it on. A high-pitched tone pierced the classroom air, getting higher and higher in frequency as the machine charged to full power. Melvin typed some last-minute calculations into the keyboard on the side of the Combine-O-Tron 2000 as its laser extractor warmed up.

Suddenly, two streaks of red glowing light flashed on to Sulu and the tiny robot. The Combine-O-Tron 2000 began assimilating information on the two elements it was about to combine. "Don't worry, kids," said Melvin. "This procedure is totally painless. Sulu won't feel a thing." Finally, a computerized voice started the countdown:

"Combining two elements in five seconds.
Combining two elements in four seconds.
Combining two elements in three seconds.
Combining two elements in two seconds.
Combining two elements in one second."

BLAZZZZT!

A burst of brilliant white light shot out of the Combine-O-Tron 2000 and formed a ball of energy between Sulu and the tiny robot. The hamster and the robot began to slide closer and closer together until they disappeared into the energy ball.

The smell of burned matches and pickle
relish filled the air as hot blasts of electric
wind knocked books off shelves and sent
papers flying. Suddenly, there was a blinding
flash of light, a quick puff of smoke, and it
was all over.

Melvin pulled off his goggles. No longer were a hamster and a robot sitting on the cart before him. Now the hamster and robot were one. Combined at a cellular level. The world's first self-contained, warm-blooded, fuzzy bionic cyborg.

"EUREKA!" shouted Melvin. "IT WORKED! I have created a cybernetic life-form."

The children looked on as Melvin waved a metal detector over the hamster and the reading went off the chart. One of the children raised his hand with a question.

"Yes!" said Melvin enthusiastically.

"Can we go to the lunchroom and get our ketchup packs now?"

"Bu – NO!" screamed Melvin. "Will you forget about Squishies for ONE MINUTE?!!? I've just created the world's first cybernetic hamster, and nobody is leaving this room until I've demonstrated his undying obedience!"

CHAPTER 4
BAD SULU

Sulu didn't seem to know that he had just undergone a groundbreaking transformation. He didn't act any different. He just wandered across the top of the plastic rolling cart sniffing everything around him, only stopping occasionally to scratch his ears or rub his whiskers. But poor Sulu was in for a big surprise.

"Sulu," said Melvin, "I am your master, and you will obey my commands. I want you to demonstrate your new powers for the class. Do a super-bionic jump across the room."

Sulu did not respond.

SNiFF
SNiFF

"Sulu!" said Melvin sternly. "Crush that plastic rolling cart in your bare paws!"

Sulu did not respond.

"SULU!" Melvin shouted. "Go outside, pick up a car, and throw it across the parking lot!"

Sulu did not respond.

Finally, Melvin reached into his book bag and took out a red Ping-Pong paddle he had designed especially for this occasion. "Sulu," he said angrily, "do as I say, or you're going to get a good spanking!"

This time, Sulu did
respond. When he saw the Ping-Pong paddle
he became very frightened, and his little
hamster instincts took over. Sulu jumped
into the air, grabbed the Ping-Pong paddle in
his right paw, and then yanked Melvin on to
the plastic rolling cart with his left paw.

The children finally stopped thinking
about ketchup packs and toilets for a
moment and settled in to watch the show.

CHAPTER 5

THE INCREDIBLY GRAPHIC VIOLENCE CHAPTER, PART 1 (IN FLIP-O-RAMA™)

WARNING:

The following chapter contains graphic depictions of a mean little boy getting spanked by a bionic hamster. While this event is presented for humorous effect, the producers of this book acknowledge that hamster attacks are no laughing matter. If you or someone you love has been the victim of a hamster attack, we strongly urge you to get help by seeking out a local support group in your area, or by visiting www.whenhamstersattack.com.

PILKEY® BRAND
D-RAMA

HERE'S HOW IT WORKS!

STEP 1
First, place your *left* hand inside the dotted lines marked "LEFT HAND HERE". Hold the book open *flat*.

STEP 2
Grasp the *right-hand* page with your right thumb and index finger (inside the dotted lines marked "RIGHT THUMB HERE").

STEP 3
Now *quickly* flip the right-hand page back and forth until the picture appears to be *animated*.

(For extra fun, try adding your own sound-effects!)

FLIP-O-RAMA 1

(pages 369 and 371)

Remember, flip *only* page 369.
While you are flipping, be sure you
can see the picture on page 369
and the one on page 371.
If you flip quickly, the two
pictures will start to look like
<u>one</u> *animated* picture.

Don't forget to
add your own sound-effects!

LEFT HAND HERE

SPANKS FOR
THE MEMORIES

RIGHT
THUMB
HERE

RIGHT
INDEX
FINGER
HERE

SPANKS FOR
THE MEMORIES

CHAPTER 6
THE AFTERMATH

Although Sulu hadn't *really* spanked Melvin very hard, Melvin wailed and blubbered and carried on anyway.

"You're a BAD hamster!" Melvin cried. "I never want to see you again as long as I live!"

Melvin ran out of the classroom sobbing.
The rest of the class, including Ms Ribble,
followed him out laughing and chanting,
"Squish-ies, Squish-ies, Squish-ies!" But
George and Harold stayed behind to
comfort the forgotten hamster.

"Don't feel bad, Sulu," said George.
"Melvin is a real meanie!"

"Yeah," said Harold. "Do you want to
come home with us? You can live up in our
tree house."

Sulu jumped on to Harold's shoulder and licked his face. Then he jumped over to George's shoulder and licked his face, too.

"I think we've just adopted a bionic hamster," said Harold.

So George tucked their new pal into his shirt pocket, and the three friends went off to lunch.

CHAPTER 7
MR KRUPP

About that very same time, the school principal, Mr Krupp, came marching into the office in a particularly foul mood. He stopped beside Miss Anthrope's desk, huffing and puffing.

"Where's my coffee, Edith?" he shouted.

"Get it yourself, tubby!" Miss Anthrope shouted back.

"I don't need your lip today, woman!" Mr Krupp growled. "I just want my coffee and I want it NOW!"

"Well, get me a cup, too, while you're at it," Miss Anthrope growled back.

"Aaaaugh!" screamed Mr Krupp in frustration as he grabbed a newspaper and headed for the faculty restroom. Ms Ribble was standing beside the restroom door smiling and trying very hard not to laugh.

"What are *you* lookin' at?" Mr Krupp
snarled as he pushed his way past Ms Ribble
and slammed the restroom door behind
him. Inside the restroom, you could hear
the faint sound of a belt buckle jingling, a
zipper unzipping, some clothes rustling,
and finally…

SPLAT!!! SPLAT!!!

"WHAT THE –!" screamed Mr Krupp from inside the restroom. "I'VE GOT KETCHUP IN MY UNDERWEAR!!!"

In a few moments, the door of the faculty restroom flew open. "I'm going to get George and Harold for this!" Mr Krupp screamed.

"They didn't do it," laughed Ms Ribble. "I did! It's called a *Squishy*. It's the latest fad!"

"Yeah, right. Very funny!" said Mr Krupp. "Now, where are those two kids? I just *KNOW* they're responsible!"

As Mr Krupp headed for the cafeteria, he noticed that he wasn't the only person to fall victim to the dreaded Squishies. All through the hallway, angry first, second, third, fifth and sixth graders were complaining about ketchup stains on their pants, socks, legs and underwear. Mr Krupp stormed into the cafeteria and headed for the fourth graders' table.

"George and Harold!" shouted Mr Krupp. "I've got ketchup in my underwear because of you two. And so do half of the kids in this school!"

"We didn't do it," said Harold.

"Yeah," said a few of the other fourth graders. "George and Harold are innocent."

"Oh no they're NOT," said a voice from
the other end of the table. It was Melvin
Sneedly. Besides being the school brainiac,
Melvin was also famous for being the school
tattletale. "George and Harold taught everybody a trick today where you put ketchup
packs under a toilet seat and make it spray
on people's legs," Melvin reported proudly.

"Thank you, Melvin," said Mr Krupp. He
turned to George and Harold and pointed at
the cafeteria door. "Mr Beard and Mr
Hutchins – OUT!"

382

CHAPTER 8

THE COMIC IS MIGHTIER THAN THE SPITBALL

George and Harold were sent straight to the detention room.

"Man," said Harold, "Melvin is such a tattletale. Somebody ought to teach him a lesson."

"And we're just the guys to do it," said George.

DETENTION

So George and Harold created an all-new comic book featuring everybody's favourite tattletalin' meanie, Melvin Sneedly. When they were done, the two boys sneaked out of the detention room to run off copies of their latest work and sell them in the hallway.

The new comic book was a great
success. Everybody loved it. Well, everybody but Melvin Sneedly, I should say. As
Melvin walked to his last class of the day,
he noticed small groups of students in
the hallway reading comics together and
giggling. Normally, this was enough to
make Melvin run straight to the principal's
office and tell on everyone for unsupervised
reading (which was strictly forbidden). But
today, Melvin noticed something strange.
The comic-reading students were pointing
and laughing – at HIM.

"What?" said Melvin. "What's wrong? What are you guys laughing at?" Melvin looked around the hallway desperately. Everybody was laughing . . . everybody was pointing . . . and it was driving Melvin crazy! He marched over to a group of second graders, grabbed the comic book out of their hands, and looked at the cover. Melvin was FURIOUS!

"YOU GUYS ARE *SO* IMMATURE!!!"
shrieked Melvin. He quickly darted off to
read the comic in peace, but everywhere he
ran, he came across more pointing and more
laughing. Finally, Melvin thought of the one
place he could read the comic in private. He
went into the boys' bathroom, locked himself
in one of the stalls, and sat down to read.

SPLAT!!! SPLAT!!!

As Melvin sat reading, his legs dripping with ketchup, he became angrier and angrier. "I'm gonna get George and Harold!" Melvin vowed.

CHAPTER 9

CAPTAIN UNDERPANTS AND THE TERRIFYING TALE OF THE TATTLE-TRON 2000

BY GEORGE BEARD AND HAROLD HUTCHINS

CAPTAIN UNDERPANTS
AND THE TERIFYING TALE
OF THE TATTLE-TRON 2000

By George Beard and Harold Hutchins

Onse upon a time There was a dumb Kid named Melvin who was a big Tattle-Tale.

I'm Telling

KEEP OFF THE GRASS

Everywhare He went he caused Greif and Mizery.

I'm Telling

NO SKATE BORDING

Until one Day...

BANK

I'm Telling

$

CRASH

Hey cops, That guy Just Robed the Bank.

Gee thanks Kid.

$

You're are under a rest.

Hey kid you solved the crime of the senchery!

PRESS

And so...

Daily News

Dumb Kid is a Hero

Everybody Loves Melvin!!!

Melvin had became so populer that he desided to run for Mayer.

Melvin 4 Mayer

Vote 4 melvin

I'm Telling

CON-FETY

Melvin 4 Mayer

My Hero

VOTE 4 A HERO

He won in a Landslide Victery

Daily News

Dumb Kid Becomes Mayer

Congrajew-lashons!!! Your the Youngest Mayer ever!

Yes and I'm going to make some BiG changes!

Mayer

Soon mayer Melvin made a bunch of Dumb new Laws.

And people were getting aRested LeFt and Right

And they all got sent to Jail

But Captain Under-pants was faster than a speeding waistband...

More Powerful Than Boxer shorts...

And able To Leap Tall Buildings Without getting a wedgie.

captain Underpants wanted to fight the Robot but he dident want to hurt the people inside.

Then he got a idea.

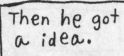

CRASH!!!

"It makes you go poop"

Hey!

What the ???

UH-OH

soon There was no-
Body Left inside
The Tattle-Tron 2000
Exsept For melvin.

CHAPTER 10

MAD MR MELVIN

Melvin was furious. He ripped the comic book in half and tossed it over his shoulder. Then he washed his hands in the toilet and stormed out of the restroom.

"I'm gonna get George and Harold for that," said Melvin. "I'm gonna teach them a lesson they'll NEVER forget!"

After school, Melvin grabbed his Combine-O-Tron 2000 and headed home.

Melvin's mother and father were both busy working on a top-secret government experiment when Melvin walked in the front door.

"Hello, son," said Melvin's father. "How was your day at school?"

"Terrible!" said Melvin. "Nobody in school has sufficient respect for my beautiful mind. Those dull-witted, lame-brained, gum-chewing idiots are more impressed with comic books than they are with the wonders of science. But I shall teach them. I shall teach them all! Ha-ha-ha-ha-haaaa!"

"That's nice, honey," said Melvin's mum.

Melvin marched up to his room to begin
building a brand-new super-powered robot.
But when he opened his bedroom door, he
saw the family's pet cat, Danderella, sleeping
quietly on his bed.

"Hey!" Melvin screamed. "What are you
doing in my room, you stupid cat? You know
I'm allergic to you! Now get out and – a – a –
A-Chooo! – STAY OUT!"

After a few hours, Melvin had built his newest and most powerful robot ever, which had three sets of interchangeable laser eyeballs, Macro-Hydraulic Jump-A-Tronic legs, Super-Somgobulating Automo-Arms, and an extendable Octo-Claw rib cage, and was powered by three separate Twin Turbo-9000 SP5 Kung-Fu Titanium/Lithium Alloy Processors, which were all built into a virtually indestructible Flexo-Growmonic endoskeleton that had the power to punch through cinder blocks, crush steel in its vice-like grasp, and plough mercilessly through poorly written run-on sentences.

It could also slice bagels.

"That ought to do the trick," said Melvin, wiping his nose on a tissue. "Now, all I have to do is – a – a – A-Chooo! – combine my body with this bionic robot, and I shall be the most powerful boy who – a – a – A-Chooo! – ever lived!"

CHAPTER 11

MELVIN'S FANTASY

As Melvin set up the Combine-O-Tron 2000 and made the proper adjustments, he imagined what his life would be like as the world's first bionic boy. He imagined himself walking into school the next day, his arms swinging confidently as he crashed through the classroom wall.

The girls would swoon as Melvin talked for hours about the amazing world of science. Ms Ribble would probably let Melvin sit at her desk from now on, because Melvin's new buns of steel would be too massive to fit into an ordinary children's chair.

Maybe Mr Krupp would invite the governor to visit the school, so he could show off his smartest and most powerful student. If so, the governor would probably declare a new holiday, "National Melvin Sneedly Day": a day when kids all over the world would get extra homework and pop quizzes to honour the glorious name of Melvin.

But the best part of all would be George and Harold's reaction. They would be so terrified by Melvin's incredible size and strength, they'd drop to their knees and beg for mercy. And Melvin would spare them only if they agreed to be his slaves for all eternity. They'd have to carry his books, sharpen his pencils, and be his personal footstools during each class.

"Life is gonna – a – a – A-Chooo! – RULE!" said Melvin.

CHAPTER 12

THE NIGHT OF THE NASTY NOSTRIL NUGGETS

Melvin turned on the Combine-O-Tron 2000. A high-pitched tone pierced the air, getting higher and higher in frequency as the machine charged to full power. "Oops," said Melvin as he quickly turned the *Dramatic Effects* setting to "off" so he wouldn't disturb his parents. Silently, the machine continued to charge as Melvin entered calculations to account for his clothes and glasses. When the laser extractor had finally warmed up, Melvin stepped in front of the Combine-O-Tron 2000, standing perfectly still beside his new robot.

Suddenly, two streaks of red glowing light flashed on to Melvin and the robot as the Combine-O-Tron 2000 began assimilating information on the two elements it was about to combine. Finally, a computerized voice started the countdown:

"**Combining two elements in five seconds.**"
Melvin stood perfectly still.

"**Combining two elements in four seconds.**"
Melvin's nose began to twitch.

"**Combining two elements in three seconds.**"
Suddenly, Melvin felt an uncontrollable urge. He cupped his hands over his mouth and nose as his eyes squeezed closed involuntarily. "A – a – a…"

"**Combining two elements in two seconds.**"

"– A-Chooo!" Melvin looked down into his hands, which were now glistening with mucus and crusty chunks of semi-dried booglets. Instantly, the Combine-O-Tron 2000 began to recalculate the elements in its laser sights.

"Combining three elements in one second."

"THREE elements?" Melvin screamed in horror. "W-W-What's the THIRD ELEMENT???"

Quickly, Melvin's eyes darted around the room, searching for any new element that might have accidentally made its way into the sights of the laser extractor.

"WHAT'S THE THIRD ELEMENT???" he screamed again. Then he looked down into his crusty, dripping, phlegm-filled hands.

"Uh-oh," said Melvin as a blinding burst of white light enveloped him.

BLAZZZZT!

CHAPTER 13

THE NEXT DAY

The next day, Melvin didn't show up for school on time. Nobody really seemed to notice, though, because all the children were excited about show-and-tell. Almost everyone had brought in really lame stuff like books or awards, but George and Harold had something that was totally *cool*.

"Everybody remembers Sulu from yesterday, right?" said George. "Well, we took him home to live with us in our tree house."

"And we taught him the greatest trick!" said Harold.

The two boys carried Sulu over to the classroom window and opened it up. Harold pulled a large watermelon out of his book bag and showed it to Sulu.

"OK, Sulu," said George, "show everybody your new trick!"

In one swift motion, Sulu placed his mouth on to the watermelon and shoved the entire thing into his left cheek. The fourth graders were stunned.

"No, no," said Harold, "that's not the trick. The trick is what happens next!"

Sulu looked out the window and eyed a dead tree at the far end of the empty playground. Sulu began to chew up the watermelon, then puckered his tiny hamster lips and spat.

Ratatatatatatatatatatatatatat!

The watermelon seeds fired out of Sulu's mouth, hitting their target with expert precision. In no time at all, the dead tree at the end of the playground was reduced to a pile of twigs and sawdust. The class cheered as George and Harold petted their amazing little bionic buddy.

George and Harold didn't think that anybody could beat their show-and-tell display, but they were wrong. Because at that very moment, Melvin Sneedly was dripping down the hallway towards the classroom door. Melvin hadn't brought anything for show-and-tell. Melvin WAS the show-and-tell.

CHAPTER 14

THE UNNECESSARILY DISGUSTING CHAPTER

NOTICE:

The following chapter is
extremely gross.

To avoid nausea, projectile
vomiting, or other gastrointestinal
unpleasantries, please refrain
from eating for at least
one hour before
reading this chapter.

(You won't want to eat after
reading it, let me assure you.)

All of the fourth graders were cheering and petting Sulu as the classroom door slowly opened. A greenish, glistening behemoth entered the room, filling the air with the sounds of grinding metal gears and wet, gooey, bursting bubbles. Some of the girls screamed. Some of the boys did, too.

"You guys are *so* immature!" said the horrible beast.

At once, the children recognized the terrifying creature that stood before them.

"MELVIN?!!?" they cried.

"Yes, it's me," gurgled the wet, jiggling monster angrily. His eyes and nose were dripping with warm, greenish, custard-like mucus. His robotic arms were caked with massive globs of crispy, shimmering snot. And as he turned to close the classroom door behind him, part of his hand came off on the doorknob. It oozed slowly down the door, leaving behind a chunky trail of moist excretion.

Melvin squished and sloshed as he jiggled over to his chair. Each gooey footstep coated the floor with a foamy trail of slime, and everything he touched became wet and encrusted with warm, bubbling, syrupy phlegm.

When Melvin sat down, generous helpings of yellowish, pudding-like goo slowly dribbled down the chair, collecting into creamy,

gelatinous puddles beneath him. The puddles themselves were slightly transparent and speckled with thick, shimmering nose hairs and dark red chunks of coagulated blood, which—

"ALL RIGHT ALREADY!" yelled George to the narrator. "Enough with the descriptions you're making us all sick!"

"Thank you, George," said Ms Ribble. "Now, Melvin, why don't you tell us all what happened to you?"

"Well," said Melvin, "I tried to combine myself with a bionic robot last night, but I accidentally sneezed at the last second."

"So you got combined with a robot — and *boogers*?" asked George.

"Yeah," said Melvin. "But don't worry, I'm building a Separatron 1000, which will reverse the effects and turn me back into a boy again. It'll just take six months to finish."

"Six *MONTHS*?" said Harold.

"Hey, cellular separation is a highly complex procedure," said Melvin. "It's not like building a robot. It takes time!"

"You should try taking the batteries out of that Combine-O-Thingy and putting them in backwards," suggested George. "That might reverse the effect."

Melvin rolled his thick, bubbling, crust-covered infra-red eyeballs. "That's the dumbest thing I've ever heard!" he gurgled.

CHAPTER 15
THE NEW MELVIN

You might think that turning into a Bionic Booger Boy was the worst thing that could ever happen to a kid, but it wasn't all bad. Believe it or not, there was actually a positive side to being a lumbering loogie lad. For instance, Melvin now won every football game he played . . . because no one wanted to tackle him.

And when he served a volleyball, nobody
on the other team would dare to hit the
ball back.

Besides being the school's new sports star, there were other perks, too. Melvin never had to wait in line at the drinking fountain any more. Now he had his own *personal* drinking fountain, because . . . well, would *you* use a drinking fountain after a Bionic Booger Boy had globbered all over it?

I didn't think so.

All of the special attention that Melvin was receiving made some of the other kids a little jealous. But not George and Harold. Considering the many evil villains that George and Harold had been battling all year, the two boys were just grateful that Melvin hadn't turned himself into a gigantic, terrifying beast with plans to destroy the earth.

"It could be a LOT worse," said Harold.
"At least Melvin's not a terrifying evil villain."
"Yeah, you're right," said George. "I can't
think of *anything* that could turn Melvin
into a terrifying evil villain… "

CHAPTER 16
THE COLD AND FLU SEASON

Soon it was autumn, and the new season brought with it many changes: crisp, chilly air; early morning frost; and bright, colourful leaves. But with the beauty of autumn came another change that wasn't quite so welcome: *the cold and flu season*.

All through Jerome Horwitz Elementary School, people were getting sick. The hallways were filled with runny noses, sneezing mouths and aching bodies.

And unfortunately, one of those
noses, mouths and bodies belonged to Melvin
Sneedly.

Every time Melvin sneezed, thousands
of tiny driblets shot out of his mouth,

spattering the chalkboard with a thin
layer of foamy, glistening, yellowish-green,
tapioca-like mucus.

"Don't forget to cover your mouth,
Melvin, dear," said Ms Ribble.

431

"Oh, sorry," said Melvin. "Sorry." He put his hand over his mouth and sneezed again. This time, the explosion of air from his stifled sneeze blew off large, wet globs of his body, which sprayed over the entire classroom.

It was as if somebody set off a giant fire-cracker inside a bucket of green paint. The warm, smelly goo smacked into people's hair, splattered on to their clothes, and seemed to drench every square centimetre of the room.

"On second thoughts, Melvin," said Ms Ribble, "*don't* cover your mouth next time. Now, who wants a cookie?"

CHAPTER 17
THE FIELD TRIP

The next day, for some strange reason, Ms Ribble was off sick with a cold. Mr Krupp was filling in as the substitute teacher and, as usual, he was very angry.

"What the *heck* is going on in this room?" he yelled. "What's with all the raincoats and umbrellas?"

Then Melvin sneezed.

A few moments later, Mr Krupp returned to the classroom with fresh clothes, a raincoat and an umbrella. "All right everybody," he shouted. "Today is Field Trip Day. Miss Anthrope and I are taking you all to Snoddy Bros. Tissue Factory to see how blow-rags are made."

The word "tissue" made Melvin jump. "NO!" he cried in a panic. "ME NO LIKE TISSUES!"

An eerie silence fell over the classroom. Everybody looked at Melvin in shock.

"Did Melvin just say *me no like tissues*?" asked Harold.

"Yeah," said George. "I've never heard him misuse an objective pronoun before. Who does he think he is, *Frankenstein*?"

CHAPTER 18

THINGS GET BAD

In a few hours, the fourth graders were all packed into a hot, stinky factory listening to a boring speech about how trees are turned into tissues . . . or something like that. Nobody was paying attention, really, except for Melvin Sneedly, who was terrified. His whole body shook and shimmered as the tour took them down the narrow walkways of the noisy industrial plant.

Finally, the tour ended at the gift shop, where the plant manager, Mr Snoddy, had a surprise for everybody.

"Behind this red curtain with black dots on it," said Mr Snoddy, "is a free gift for each of you." Mr Snoddy pulled back the curtain to reveal a pile of sample tissue packs. "Help yourselves," said Mr Snoddy. "There's enough for everybody!"

"NOOOOO!" screamed Melvin. "ME NO LIKE TISSUES!"

"Oh, don't be silly," said Mr Snoddy. "Everybody *loves* tissues. And our tissues are extra absorbent. They really help to wipe out phlegm and mucus!"

"NOOOOO!" screamed Melvin again. "TISSUES IS *BAD MAGIC*!"

"Nonsense," laughed Mr Snoddy. He tossed a couple of sample tissue packs at Melvin. "Here you go, young man," he said. "Enjoy!"

The tissue packs flipped through the air and stuck on to Melvin's back. Melvin screamed. His eyes began to glow green as he beat his chest in anger. Suddenly, Melvin's shoulders started to bubble. His chest expanded. The Flexo-Growmonic steel in Melvin's endoskeleton flexed and grew. His neck and head widened, and his body swelled to a height of four metres.

Melvin grabbed the tissue packs in his
massive, dripping fingers and flung them
to the ground. "DON'T MAKE ME ANGRY!"
Melvin warned. "YOU NO LIKE ME WHEN
I ANGRY!"

"Oops," said Mr Snoddy. "You dropped
your tissue packs, young fellow. Here's some
more for you!" Mr Snoddy grabbed two giant
handfuls of sample tissue packs and tossed
them at Melvin.

CHAPTER 19
THINGS GET BADDER

Frantically, Melvin swatted at the nine new tissue packs stuck to his upper torso as if they were a swarm of stinging bumblebees. He stomped his giant spiked feet and thrashed about violently as his hulking body doubled, then *tripled* in size. Melvin kicked and punched the walls of the gift shop as he let out a terrifying, bloodcurdling cry.

"There's no need to cry, little man," said Mr Snoddy. "Here – have some more tissues to dry those tears!" He tossed several more sample tissue packs at Melvin. (As you might have noticed by now, Mr Snoddy wasn't exactly the brightest bulb on the Hanukkah tree.)

444

What happened next could only be
described as chaos. Once again, Melvin's
massive body tripled in size. By now, Melvin
was roaring and kicking and knocking over
giant machines. Children screamed and ran.

445

Mr Snoddy thought it might help matters if he could just give Melvin some more tissues. But before he could, a drop of mucus the size of a bathtub dripped from Melvin's massive nose and splashed down on Mr Snoddy, gluing him to the floor.

George and Harold hid behind the red curtain with black dots on it as Melvin crashed through the roof of the factory. Ear-piercing roars bellowed out of his gigantic, oozing mouth as he kicked down the walls of the factory and tossed heavy machinery into the parking lot. Mr Krupp and Miss Anthrope tried their best to get the situation under control, but they weren't having much luck.

"Hey, bub," shouted Mr Krupp, "I've had just about enough of your shenanigans!"

"You're gonna be spending the afternoon in detention if you don't settle down, young man!" shouted Miss Anthrope.

Suddenly, Melvin reached down and
grabbed Miss Anthrope in his massive
metal fist.

"HELP ME!" she screamed. "SOMEBODY
SAVE ME!"

"Uh … ummm …" said Mr Krupp
nervously, "I'll – I'll go get some help!"

Mr Krupp ran and hid with George and Harold behind the red curtain with black dots on it.

"Hey, I thought you were going to go get some help!" said Harold.

"Well, not *today*," said Mr Krupp.

"You know," said George, "there's only one person who can help Miss Anthrope now."

"Who's that?" asked Mr Krupp.

CHAPTER 20

CAPTAIN UNDERPANTS, THAT'S WHO

As much as George and Harold hated to do it, they decided that it was time to send in Captain Underpants to save the day. George snapped his fingers. Suddenly, the terror and panic that Mr Krupp had been experiencing completely vanished.

A wild, silly grin spread across his face as he leaped to his feet and ripped off his outer clothing and toupee. Mr Krupp's transformation into Captain Underpants was almost complete. The only thing he was missing was a cape.

"Gee," he said, "I sure wish I could find a red curtain with black dots on it."

"Hey," said George as he pointed to the red curtain with black dots on it, "here's a red curtain with black dots on it."

"What a remarkably unexpected coincidence," said Captain Underpants as he grabbed the latest in a series of convoluted plot devices and tied it around his neck.

By this time, Melvin had stomped his way
out of the factory and into the downtown
area, leaving behind a twisted path of mucus-
coated destruction. Captain Underpants flew
into the air, following the trail of terror until
he was face-to-face with the snot-spewing
cyborg.

"I order you to stop," said Captain
Underpants, "in the name of all that is Pre-
Shrunk and Cottony!" Melvin did not listen.

Captain Underpants had no choice but to fight the boogery behemoth, but first he needed to save Miss Anthrope. Quickly, our hero flew to Edith's side, grabbed her hands, and pulled firmly. The slimy phlegm that covered Melvin's gigantic fist was strong and gluey, but it was no match for Wedgie Power.

Captain Underpants pulled and pulled until Miss Anthrope became completely dislodged with a noisy, wet, disgusting sound. (Note: Please feel free to make the noisy, wet, disgusting sound of your choice to emphasize the intense drama of this gripping paragraph.)

"I'm free!" cried Miss Anthrope. "Let's get the heck out of here!"

Suddenly, the Bionic Booger Boy reached down and grabbed Captain Underpants by the cape. The monster held on tightly with his gigantic, gooey robotic fingers.

"ACK!" cried Captain Underpants. "He's got my cape! He's got my cape!"

"Well just untie it!" screamed Miss Anthrope. "Let's GO! Let's GO!"

"But I – I can't fight crime without my cape!" cried Captain Underpants.

"FORGET YOUR STUPID CAPE!" Edith screamed. "Just save me, you idiot!"

CHAPTER 21

YOU CAN'T HAVE YOUR CAPE AND EDITH, TOO

As anybody will tell you, no superhero is complete without a cape. I mean, without a cape, a superhero is just a guy wearing fancy underwear (or in this case, *not*-so-fancy underwear). But Captain Underpants knew what had to be done. He reached up with his free hand and courageously untied his cape, valiantly sacrificing his aesthetic integrity to save the life of a mere mortal being.

Captain Underpants and Miss Anthrope
were now free, but they weren't safe yet.
The Bionic Booger Boy swung at our hero
with all his might. Captain Underpants
weaved around Melvin's frantic, flying,
phlegm-flingin' fists as he tried to find a
safe place to land.

459

Suddenly, Captain Underpants's 100% cotton-powered vision spotted George and Harold miles away. With lightning speed, he flew down to meet the boys.

"George and Harold," said Captain Underpants, "you've got to keep this woman safe while I destroy that robotic slimeball!"

"OK," said Harold, "but hurry up — here he comes!"

"Wait," cried Miss Anthrope. "I – I didn't get a chance to say thank you." She turned and kissed Captain Underpants all over his face with wet, drooly smooches.

"Thank you! Thank you! Thank you!" she said between each sloppy kiss.

"Yuck!" said Harold.

"I sure hope she doesn't thank *us*," said
George.

When Miss Anthrope had finished
slobbering all over Captain Underpants's face,
she gave him a great big hug for good luck.
"Now go get him, tiger," she said coyly.

But Captain Underpants didn't move. He
just stood there staring blankly into space.

Off in the distance, George and Harold
could hear the Bionic Booger Boy approach-
ing. Each thundering footstep brought the
horrible beast closer and closer, until at last
he stood towering above them, panting
heavily, and dripping profanely.

Miss Anthrope screamed and ran away.

"Hurry, Captain Underpants!" cried
Harold. "DO SOMETHING!"

"Yeah," cried George. "KICK HIS
BACKSIDE! KICK HIS BACKSIDE!"

But Captain Underpants didn't move. He
didn't fight. He didn't fly. He didn't kick
anybody's backside. In fact, the only thing he
did do was get very, very angry.

"What the heck is going on here, bubs?"
he screamed. "And why am I standing here
in my underwear?"

George and Harold didn't like the sound
of that.

464

CHAPTER 22

WELCOME BACK, KRUPPER

If you read the comic on page 7 of this novel, then you know what happens whenever Captain Underpants gets water on his head. Unfortunately, Miss Anthrope's wet, slobbery kisses had produced the same effect.

Captain Underpants had been turned back into Mr Krupp . . . and now he was about to be turned into *lunch*!

Quickly, George and Harold began
frantically snapping their fingers.

SNAP! SNAP! SNAP! SNAP! SNAP!

Again and again, they snapped. But Mr
Krupp's face was still slimy and wet with
gooey kiss juice, and the snaps were
having no effect at all.

The mighty mucus monster shoved Mr
Krupp into his gummy mouth and swallowed
him whole . . .

. . . and then he came after George and
Harold.

"HELP!" screamed George.

"WE'RE DOOMED!" screamed Harold.

CHAPTER 23
SULU SAVES THE DAY

Halfway across the city, a plucky little hamster with bionic ears heard the terrified cries of his two best pals. Quickly, Sulu jumped out of his exercise wheel and crashed through the side of his plastic cage.

Then, with a mighty leap, he bounded from the window of George and Harold's tree house.

At that very moment, Melvin was dangling George and Harold high above his mouth.

"HAW, HAW, HAW!" laughed the Bionic Booger Boy. "ME GOTS YOU AT LAST!"

"Well, goodbye, Harold," said George.

"See you later, pal," said Harold. "It was fun while it lasted."

Finally, Melvin let go of George and Harold. The two boys screamed as they fell face first into the gooey, gaping mouth of the—

SWOOOOOOOOOOOOSH!

The next thing George and Harold knew,
they were flying sideways at an incredible
speed. Everything around them was a blur
of motion, except for the sight of their little
buddy Sulu, who had literally grabbed them
from the murky mouth of death at the very
last second.

"Atta boy!" cried George.

"Hooray for Sulu!" cried Harold.

471

Sulu set George and Harold down on the
roof of a distant building, then returned to
the scene of the crime. He grabbed a few
oversize novelty items from the tops of
some warehouses and turned to face his
mortal enemy.

THE CANE
WAREHOUSE

BOXING
GLOVE CITY

THE DENT
EMPORIU

CHAPTER 24

THE INCREDIBLY GRAPHIC VIOLENCE CHAPTER, PART 2 (IN FLIP-O-RAMA™)

WARNING:

The following stunts were
performed on closed streets
by a highly trained
professional hamster.
To avoid injury,
please do not grab
oversize novelty items
from the tops of
warehouses and beat up
giant monsters
with them.

FLIP-O-RAMA 2

(pages 475 and 477)

Remember, flip *only* page 475.
While you are flipping, be sure you
can see the picture on page 475
and the one on page 477.
If you flip quickly, the two
pictures will start to look like
<u>one</u> *animated* picture.

Don't forget to
add your own sound-effects!

LEFT HAND HERE

CANE TOPS KEEP
FALLIN' ON MY HEAD

475

RIGHT
THUMB
HERE

RIGHT
INDEX
FINGER
HERE

CANE TOPS KEEP
FALLIN' ON MY HEAD

FLIP-O-RAMA 3

(pages 479 and 481)

Remember, flip *only* page 479.
While you are flipping, be sure you
can see the picture on page 479
and the one on page 481.
If you flip quickly, the two
pictures will start to look like
<u>one</u> *animated* picture.

Don't forget to
add your own sound-effects!

LEFT HAND HERE

YUMMY, YUMMY, YUMMY (I GOT GLOVE IN MY TUMMY)

479

RIGHT THUMB HERE

RIGHT
INDEX
FINGER
HERE

YUMMY, YUMMY, YUMMY (I GOT GLOVE IN MY TUMMY)

FLIP-O-RAMA 4

(pages 483 and 485)

Remember, flip *only* page 483.
While you are flipping, be sure you
can see the picture on page 483
and the one on page 485.
If you flip quickly, the two
pictures will start to look like
<u>one</u> *animated* picture.

Don't forget to
add your own sound-effects!

LEFT HAND HERE

A HARD DAY'S BITE

RIGHT
THUMB
HERE

RIGHT
INDEX
FINGER
HERE

A HARD DAY'S BITE

CHAPTER 25

HOW TO REVERSE THE EFFECTS OF A COMBINE-O-TRON 2000 IN ONE EASY STEP

The Bionic Booger Boy was defeated. He flopped, unconscious, into a giant boogery blob that spread across several city blocks (and nearly four whole pages) as reporters surrounded his massive, oozing body.

Soon, Melvin's mother and father showed up with the Combine-O-Tron 2000. "We saw what was happening on the news," they said. "And we want the world to know that we're going to create a new machine that will reverse the process that turned our son into this monster. If we work together, it should only take a few months to build!"

"Why don't you guys just take the batteries out of that *Combine-O-Thingy* and switch 'em around?" said George. "Wouldn't that reverse the machine's effects?"

"Well," laughed Melvin's father, "obviously you don't know anything about science, little boy. You can't expect to reverse the effects of a highly complex cellular-moleculizing Combine-O-Tron just by switching the batteries around. That type of thing only happens in obnoxious children's books."

"Ahem," said George self-consciously. "Well . . . why don't you just give it a try anyway?"

"All right," said Mr Sneedly, rolling his eyes and smirking. He quickly switched the batteries around and powered up the machine. "But I'm only doing this to prove a point to you kids: It's not gonna work. No way. Not in a million years. And anybody who thinks it might is a complete idiot. It goes against all the popular laws of logic and science."

He aimed the newly reconfigured Combine-O-Tron 2000 at his son and fired.

CHAPTER 26
BLAZZZZT!

Suddenly, there was a terrific explosion.
The Bionic Booger Boy burst into three huge
chunks of glistening snot and twisted metal,
which smacked on to three nearby buildings
and stuck like glue. In the centre of the
explosion, surrounded by smoke, stood Mr
Krupp and Melvin.

"Well, what do you know?" said Mr
Sneedly. "My idea worked."

George and Harold rolled their eyes.

"Now, step aside, kiddies," said Mrs Sneedly as the two scientists marched off to tell the reporters all about their brilliant and inspirational scientific breakthrough.

But as the smoke around Mr Krupp and Melvin began to clear, it became obvious that they were not quite back to normal. Apparently, the newly reconfigured Combine-O-Tron 2000 had accidentally morphed Mr Krupp and Melvin together.

"Don't worry," Mr Sneedly told the reporters. "All I need to do is zap them one more time. That should set everything straight!" He fired up the Combine-O-Tron 2000 again and prepared to blast away.

"I sure hope this separates their bodies," said George.

"Me, too," said Harold.

BLAZZZZT!

CHAPTER 27

TO MAKE A LONG STORY SHORT

It did.

CHAPTER 28
A HAPPY ENDING

"You know something?" said George. "This is the first time one of our books actually had a happy ending."

"You're right," said Harold. "Usually they end with you screaming 'Oh, NO!' and me screaming 'Here we go again!' But we got lucky this time, I guess."

"What do you mean, *lucky*?" said Mr
Krupp. "It was *MY* invention that saved the
world. You guys are *so* immature!"

"Huh?" said George.

"I want to see both of you bubs in my office PRONTO!" yelled Melvin. "I'm gonna punish you boys so bad, your *kids* will be born with detentions!"

"Whaaaa?" said Harold.

Suddenly, a giant extendable Octo-Claw
reached out from one of the three huge
chunks of boogers. It grabbed the Combine-
O-Tron 2000 out of Mr Sneedly's hands and
smashed it to smithereens on the ground.
Mr and Mrs Sneedly ran away screaming
as the three humongous robotic booger
chunks came to life.

Slowly, they began dripping down the sides of the buildings, each one energizing itself with a single Twin Turbo-9000 SP5 Kung-Fu Titanium/Lithium Alloy Processor.

As the huge booger chunks oozed closer
and closer, they began sprouting strange-
looking metallic eyeballs and huge,
menacing robotic limbs.

Suddenly, the three Ridiculous Robo-
Boogers leaped towards George, Harold,
Sulu, Mr Krupp and Melvin . . .

. . . and the chase was on.

"Oh, NO!" screamed George.

"Here we go again!" screamed Harold.

Look out for...